Greenwood

In the end, we are all residents of Greenwood, bound and connected by the imperfect fabric of our shared humanity.

Mark Morrow

Mark Morrow
Copyright © 2023 Mark Morrow
Summer House Books

All rights reserved. This book may not be reproduced in any form, in whole or in part (beyond the copying permitted by US Copyright Law, Section 107, "fair use" in teaching or research, Section 108, certain library copying, or in published media by reviewers in limited excerpts), without written permission from the author.

This is a work of fiction. Names, characters, businesses, places, events, locales, and incidents are either the products of the author's imagination or used in a fictitious manner. Any resemblance to actual persons, living or dead, or actual events is purely coincidental.

For permission requests, email the author at msfixer@gmail.com

Paperback ISBN: 979-8-218-28794-8
Ebook ISBN: 979-8-218-30926-8

Library of Congress Control Number: 2023918164

Cover and interior design by Deborah Perdue, Illumination Graphics
Stock art courtesy of shutterstock.com and depositphotos.com

DEDICATION

For Tally,
my best friend and soulmate
and for my adventurous and fearless children,
Olivia and Camille.
I love you all dearly.

Contents

Preface - 1

1 – Consequences - 7

2 – Greenwood - 27

3 – Dumbo Gets His Day - 50

4 – Marilee's Fishpond - 67

5 – Sara Jean's Bees - 96

6 – Valerie Jean Smith - 112

7 – Weston's Big Breakfast - 138

8 – A Game of Chess - 154

9 – Henry Lee's Bird - 172

10 – Milton Gets His Freedom - 190

About the Author - 204

Preface

SOME YEARS AGO, CORMAC MCCARTHY GAVE ME this advice about writing fiction and the difficulty of doing it well.

> "It's a peculiar thing," he wrote in response to a short story I had sent him. "I think you'll have to write some more before you're fully tuned into the I that writes. *Some* writers with a body of work behind them and some considerable reputations never have done it. They can write an essay in good sensible English, but as soon as they sit down to write fiction something strange happens to them, and they begin to speak in tongues. Only a literary person could read their stuff. Children and dogs know immediately that it's bogus."

Cormac and I eventually stopped corresponding as he became more famous and sought after, and I moved on to other projects, but I was sad we were not able to reconnect before he died in 2023.

Still, his observation about writing fiction rings true, especially his assertion that "bogus" attempts to create fictional narratives are easy to spot. Perhaps that is one reason I have avoided for the most part any further public airing of my fiction, something I realize is a thinly veiled, cowardly attempt to avoid the kindly letdown my friend Cormac delivered while he was in the midst of finishing up what many critics consider his finest work, *Blood Meridian*.

The more mundane reason I abandoned fiction writing is a purely practical one. I needed to make a living. The results of that choice, for better or worse, are documented in miles of newsprint and magazine galleys where my journalistic efforts appeared over the years and in the pages of the dozens of books I edited, developed, or ghostwrote for the most part, nearly all of them nonfiction. That was then; this is now.

The reason "now" is different is due to a fiction writing group I joined more than ten years ago in Alexandria, Virginia. The group, formed by a local award-winning novelist, Leslie Pietrzyk, is a comforting, supportive refuge for aspiring fiction writers trying to find their voice. The group met, at least until COVID times, the second Wednesday of every month at a local restaurant where we'd buy a round of coffee and/or breakfast pastries while we chitchatted in anticipation of settling down to the happy but serious business of making stuff up.

Mostly, we're a prompt-writing group. Leslie gives us a prompt (usually two), and then we write for thirty minutes anxiously dreading her "time's up" call. Then, if one of us feels the muse has given us something worth sharing, we volunteer to read out loud. It's a no-pressure group that supports the art and craft of writing. As such, we do not criticize one another's pieces and instead work hard to find even the thinnest strand of workable narrative. It's a practice of patience and grace that means we mostly read what we've written even if we don't like it much ourselves.

I have been amazed, and even awed, by what a group of writers can come up with in such a short amount of time. What is more astounding is that Leslie's simple, innocuous prompt words (window, wander, difficult, habit, patience, tree) have been the planted seeds for narratives that eventually found their way into various literary journals and/or other fiction or even nonfiction narrative collections. A good number of these creative seeds (or at least a cutting or two from a prompt's mature planting) can be found in Leslie's 2021 book, *Admit This to No One* (Unnamed Press). And now, I guess, this collection of short stories.

Greenwood is not my first published book. That book, a collection of portraits and essays called *Images of the Southern Writer* (UGA Press), is about spending time (sometimes days) with a number of the South's most recognizable writers—Tennessee Williams, Eudora Welty, Robert Penn Warren, Anne Tyler, William Styron, Lee Smith, Walker Percy, Cormac McCarthy, Barry Hannah, Ernest Gaines, James Dickey, Erskine Caldwell, and dozens of others—and was a deep dive into my literary heritage as a Southerner.

It was a book that took five years to finish as I begged and cajoled for an audience with these writers despite having no reputation as a photographer or writer and, perhaps worse, no contract or even the promise of one. How this turned around at the last minute is its own story of wholesale naivete, inexperience, blind luck, and ultimately the kindness of strangers.

And although I didn't appreciate it at the time, the years-long journey of corresponding with these writers—all the while studying their work in preparation for meeting them one day—was work that gave me a deep appreciation of both their unique voices and their outsized contribution to American literature. That profound appreciation is surely embedded in these stories and is perhaps hiding in plain sight.

The characters here are, in the most fundamental of ways, recognizably Southern. At the same time, finding their counterparts in any group of humans who gather together as a community is an easy task, whether they live in New York, Kansas, Ohio, North Dakota, Arizona, or California. To put it more directly, we are all, in one way or another, residents of Greenwood, bound and connected by the imperfect fabric of our shared humanity and subject to the same human foibles and spectacular lapses in judgment the good citizens of Greenwood sometimes exhibit.

Clearly, Merle Flack, in the story "Sara Jean's Bees," should have known better than to put an active beehive in the backseat of his car, part of a kindhearted effort to help his sister move her "fragile things" to her new home. It was an acquiescence on his part that defied all common sense given his fear of bees, a terror driven by his memory of stepping on a yellow jacket nest in the woods as a child. He still vividly remembers how it felt watching from the backseat of the family's sedan, his head resting in his mother's lap, as his father careened through the streets of Greenwood on the way to the hospital.

Larry Fine, in the story "Consequences," clearly did not consider the true cost of his one-time infidelity, a levy that grew exponentially larger when a substantial portion of the town's smug citizenry viewed an illegally obtained video of him in flagrante delicto with one of his publishing colleagues underneath a poolside clamshell daybed at a high-end Virginia Beach hotel.

And was it Robert Lee Johnson's enlightenment or naivete in the story "A Game of Chess" that convinced the straitlaced insurance agent that hiking the Appalachian Trail was a good idea? This was an especially odd choice given Robert Lee's long history of making it crystal clear that he hated absolutely everything about the wilderness whenever the subject came up—and in particular, the inescapable requirement of sleeping on the ground.

The other narrative fiber that ties these stories together is a sense of place, something often associated with Southern fiction, although this is certainly not a feeling exclusive to the region south of the Mason-Dixon Line. Few characters in the collection abandon their hometowns, and those who choose to leave and return always find a renewed sense of meaning and purpose as they settle in and become part of their native communities again.

Hamilton Green, in the signature story "Greenwood," is the great-great-grandson of the town's founder Lester Hamilton Green. Hamilton was happy to have escaped Greenwood until his aunt convinced him to return from Washington, DC, to direct the family's nonprofit foundation, an organization charged with looking after his family's ancestral mansion, a landmark that is a local tourist attraction. Hamilton ultimately finds fulfillment in his "small pond celebrity," noting that Washington was a place where his family's reputation hardly bought him "a free cup of coffee" unless one of his state senators or representatives was offering it.

After a lunch with his wife, a former Washington power broker, at Dixie's Diner in downtown Greenwood, he reflects on how simple activities, such as having lunch surrounded by the buzz of conversation among other patrons and his lively, familiar exchanges with the restaurant's owner "can unleash a flood of emotions that leaves me feeling grateful and perhaps a little sad. Gratitude on the one hand for the sweetness of my life and its meaningful, deep connections, and on the other hand, loss, regret, and sadness for abandoning the warm embrace of my family and our community for all these years."

In the collection's final story, "Milton Gets His Freedom," an adolescent boy constrained under his mother's protective thumb takes a road trip to Raleigh with his charismatic grandfather, Bentley Thomas, a sales representative for the Reynolds Tobacco Company. Bentley grew up in the state capital and was allowed to explore the city unsupervised and unconstrained by fear. Bentley hopes that by giving his grandson a similar taste of freedom—allowing him to explore the capitol grounds alone—it will release him from his mother's powerful grip and instill in him a new sense of autonomy and agency.

"Bentley's hope, as fanciful as it seemed, was that some residual of his own spirit of fearlessness, and perhaps stupidity at times, might have seeped into the surrounding soil and would, like an ancient warrior's ghost, rise up to inhabit Milton's sheltered heart."

Milton does eventually find the courage to explore the wider world and with his grandfather's sense of wonder and curiosity. This newfound connection to the wider world eventually motivates him to leave Greenwood's comfortable but ultimately limiting confines to live a more adventurous adulthood.

"Years later Milton would develop a near obsession with reading historical placards, something that compelled him to pull off the road to read them, an activity that drew him into imagining what had happened there and if something did, whether it might be good story to tell, or perhaps even something to write about."

1

Consequences

WHEN LARRY FINE BOUGHT THE LITTLE HOUSE perched on a wooded hill about two hundred yards from the highway, he didn't think his renters would mind the distant hum of traffic, a sound that reminded him of his own therapist's white noise machine or the faint sound of a faucet left running in a perfectly quiet house.

Over the years, the noise-dampening buffer of trees and vegetation on either side of the road had slowly disappeared as new lanes were added and a suburban wasteland of fast-food restaurants, big box retailers, gas stations, used car dealerships, and midrange hotels advertising all-you-can-eat Sunday buffets grew up around the house. He hardly noticed the escalation in background noise when he dropped by to collect rent from a tenant or replace a broken kitchen sink disposal.

Currently, his property line was less than seventy-five yards from the edge of the most recent excavation of the property's protective hill, the last portion of which had been scraped away only six months ago to make room for another strip mall called Creek's Edge Shopping Center. He hadn't visited any of the new stores, although he suspected he eventually would because he was living, at least for the foreseeable future, in his own run-down rental with a panoramic view of industrial trash compactors and rooftop air-conditioning units.

How he—the firstborn son of Marcus Garvey Fine, president of the Greenwood Community Bank and one of the town's most respected citizens—had ended up living in his own precariously situated rental house is a story of poor judgment that sometimes surprised even him, a fact he fully acknowledged while sitting on his porch in the evening sipping a beer.

"Damn, Larry," he said to himself, "that sure is some disappointing view you got there." He still managed to chuckle even though the joke was on him.

The fact that Larry had banished himself to the west part of Greenwood was all the more unfortunate given his family's enviable lineage. His great-grandfather, Abraham Fine, had arrived in town penniless in 1876 from Maryland and begun working for Harrison Price, a wealthy Northern tycoon who had opened a hardware store a few years earlier that competed directly with a general store owned by the town's founder, Lester Green.

If Abraham was anything, he was ambitious. He saved every penny of his meager earnings as a salesclerk in Harrison's hardware store until he could afford to buy a few acres of land just west of town. Over the course of five years, Abraham managed to acquire nearly two hundred acres of woodlands covered in pine, oak, hickory, and walnut, and in 1883 he opened Fine Lumber Company using his land holdings as collateral to buy sawmill equipment. Harrison Price was not happy with his former employee's ambition, but he ultimately congratulated Abraham on his formidable business acumen and wished him well.

Abraham soon paid off his bank note and began looking for other investments in town, mainly in real estate as the post-war economy began to boom. Larry's great-grandfather was also a strategic, forward-thinking businessman who replaced the trees he cut with seedlings—a practice no one understood at the time because the benefits lay one hundred years down the road. It was a legacy of foresight that still provided a steady stream of income to Abraham's descendants.

Eventually, Abraham established the Greenwood Community Bank, an institution catering to ambitious entrepreneurs like himself. Under Abraham's savvy management the bank prospered. For the rest of his life, every time Abraham thought about someone like him starting a bank he chuckled in amazement. "Life will just surprise you like that sometimes," he always said before putting his head down and getting back to work.

Naturally, Larry's father had assumed his oldest son would work in one of the family's businesses since Larry had demonstrated an early knack for commerce beginning with an afternoon newspaper route for the *Raleigh Times*. It was a job he loved enough to race down to the Greenwood City Hall parking lot after school to pick up his papers from Joe Hopkins, the paper's local subscription manager, who handed down heavy bundles of newspapers to Larry from his delivery van. Larry liked the smell of freshly printed papers that filled the air when Joe flung open the van doors. It was a smell that both overpowered and comforted him like the aroma shed by one of his abundantly perfumed aunts when they walked past him at family reunions.

Larry's early attraction to the newspaper business had been bolstered by his neighbor Edward P. Smith, his father's fishing buddy who just happened to be the print supervisor for the *Raleigh Times*. When Larry was in the eighth grade, Mr. Smith gave Larry a personal tour of the newspaper's print room. It was an experience that deeply impressed him as he watched that day's paper being churned out. To an adolescent boy, the press seemed to have a life force of its own and he imagined it more like an actual living, breathing creature that required constant feeding and caretaking by a squadron of subservient workers who scurried around the vibrating, belching beast like Lilliputians.

After the newspaper visit, Larry had taken his responsibilities even more seriously. He managed his payment book like an accountant, making sure the *Raleigh Times* logo faced out when he slung his canvas delivery bag across his shoulder. He was proud of his association with both the newspaper and the awesome machine that created it, a pride of association that went well beyond any satisfaction he felt about being the son of a bank president.

As richly drawn as these youthful lessons were, they now seemed taken from someone else's life, given the precarious position he found himself in, nearly fifty, separated from his wife, and estranged from his three children, Chloe, Samuel, and Thomas. And to top it off, he was living in one of his own unrenovated rental properties while the good folks of Greenwood discussed the most intimate details of his personal life as if he were a reality show contestant.

Realistically, Larry's situation was not that unusual. People were forever having their affairs exposed; their backroom, barely legal, business deals investigated; their peccadillos peeked in on; and their sexual orientations and bedroom preferences guessed about in whispered side conversations among friends and strangers alike.

He knew that most people felt mostly smug about his exposed

embarrassments, and they thanked God it had not happened to them. Unfortunately, Larry was a public figure of sorts—publisher of the *Greenwood Clarion* and the son of Marcus Garvey Fine—an association that served to increase the already rampant smugness of Greenwood's citizenry as they spoke of his downfall.

Larry knew it was trite to say, but he had never even considered having an affair before it happened, but once he crossed that unthinkable chasm, he was trapped in its consequences like a fly trapped in a honeypot helpless and unable to extricate himself. And, like many others similarly trapped, he believed a confession to his wife would somehow allow a return to his former, relatively happy life. But that was before a goodly portion of the town's populace had seen the surprisingly clear security camera footage of him in flagrante delicto with his publishing colleague Betty Ann White underneath a poolside clamshell daybed at an elegant Virginia Beach hotel.

Like most occurrences in life, it was an unfathomable alignment of circumstances that brought Betty Ann and Larry together for their poolside performance. Betty Ann's journey to the poolside stage began in Summerville, a town northeast of Raleigh toward the coast, where she was raised by good middle-class parents who sent her to Bible camp every summer as a child. She was encouraged to excel at school, which she did, graduating near the top of her class. Her parents were slightly disappointed by her decision to major in journalism, but they knew she'd make the best of it. After graduation, Betty Ann took a job as a reporter for a midsize daily newspaper in Ohio instead of somewhere closer to home, a decision her parents grudgingly accepted.

Betty Ann clawed her way up from general assignment reporter to city desk editor and then to editor in chief. She loved the work, but it was a stressful job that didn't leave much time for serious romantic relationships. As a result, she fell into a pattern of brief romances, some satisfying, some not, some longer, some shorter, but none she thought worthy of pursuing long term.

Her application for the publisher's job at her hometown newspaper, the *Summerville Tribune*, was sent in after a colleague noticed an advertisement in a professional journal and pointed it out to her, mostly as a joke.

"Hey, Betty Ann," the colleague had said at the time, "look at this." He handed the journal across her desk, pointing at the job notice he'd circled in red ink. "You're always complaining about working too hard and that you need a break. Check this job out. Sounds perfect to me, and it's in your hometown."

The colleague, with whom she'd had a brief affair when they were both reporters, smiled broadly, then added, "Not that I want you to go anywhere. I like having you around."

"Thanks, I like it here too," she said, "but maybe I'll apply anyway, just for the fun of it."

"You do that," her colleague said, "and I'll come work for you. Hone my Southern accent so I can say 'so nice to see y'all' every time I leave the room whether I mean it or not."

Betty Ann tossed the journal aside after her colleague left, but she reread the description later and tried to imagine running a small, regional daily newspaper in her hometown. At first, the idea seemed laughable as she envisioned news stories about the latest big box store grand opening and enormous banner headlines heralding award-winning pumpkins. No way, she had thought. But instead of returning the journal to her friend, she hesitated and threw it on top of her to-do pile.

The next day, she reread the job posting and then emailed a cover letter and resume to the *Tribune*. She chuckled when she clicked the send button despite knowing it was an unprofessional prank to apply for a job that she had no intention of taking. Betty Ann thought about trying to recall the email, but changed her mind, still confused about the mixture of ambivalence and excitement she felt.

Two days later, she got a message from the executive director of the *Tribune*'s board.

"Betty Ann, this is Simon Truffle calling in response to your interest in the publisher position at the *Summerville Tribune*. We would love to sit down and discuss the position with you. Is there any chance you can come down early next week?"

Betty Ann, who was between meetings and on her way back to her office, had stopped briefly in the middle of the newsroom to check messages on her phone. The message caught her off guard, and she was speechless for a moment. Then she reacted as if she were sitting on her couch at home.

"Oh, damn," she exclaimed, her body going limp, "damn . . . damn . . . damn."

Reporters in her immediate vicinity looked at one another, wondering if some national tragedy had happened, but no one chased after her as she rushed off to her office and closed the door behind her.

As it turned out, being the publisher of her hometown newspaper was still a stressful job because keeping any newspaper solvent was still a financial highwire act that even well-financed papers struggled to get right. Still, the job allowed her to go home on time most days. And with her extra time, she built a less hectic life supported and encouraged by her family and a large community of old friends and acquaintances. Mainly, everyone was just glad to finally have her home.

Greenwood

※

Larry Fine's journey to the poolside clamshell daybed was perhaps more surprising as he was someone known for his steadfast devotion to his wife, Louisa May Parker, and their three children. That's why he first claimed his affair was nothing more than a classic case of midlife crisis, more about reclaiming his youth, which he knew wasn't true.

He and his wife had done a fair amount of "wild oat sowing," as Pastor Jenkins sometimes characterized youthful exuberances and debaucheries from the pulpit of the Greenwood Methodist Church on Sunday mornings. Moreover, he and Louisa May worked hard to stay in shape and not let themselves go to seed, something many people their age allowed to happen, as if morphing into Pillsbury-dough people was a natural process that happened when a marriage had a few years on it and children came along.

No, the facts were clear; he had only himself to blame, a realization that washed over him every time he sat on his porch listening to the shopping center's air-conditioning units hum and rattle and whine in unison like a mechanical, taunting, dissonant Greek chorus.

※

The Calvin Hotel in Virginia Beach opened its doors in April 1927 to much fanfare. It was the grand dame of hostelry in the region at the time. During its first few years, the hotel garnered a reputation as a playground for the rich and famous. Authors and actors stayed there: F. Scott Fitzgerald, Bette Davis, Judy Garland, and even a few US presidents, Coolidge, Truman, Eisenhower, Kennedy, and Johnson. In 1929, a famous businessman fell to his death from the hotel's sixth floor, and over the years guests occasionally reported seeing ghostly presences on that floor.

And although hundreds, perhaps thousands, of affairs had begun in the hotel's guest rooms, closets, restrooms, storerooms, and every other imaginable place where two humans might conceivably copulate, Larry and Betty Ann's indiscretion was the first to have been filmed and shared for public viewing.

If asked, Larry and Betty Ann's conference colleagues would have said they weren't surprised to see them together at the annual publishers association conference. The meeting that year at the Calvin Hotel was nothing out of the ordinary. In fact, Larry and Betty Ann served on several committees together, including one focused on the future of newspapers in an online world.

Their friendship had begun four years earlier at a preconference cocktail party where they struck up a conversation that lasted for hours. Betty Ann liked Larry's humor: it was not unusual for them to laugh until tears ran down their cheeks. She also liked how equitably Larry treated her, how he engaged with her, and how he clearly respected her opinions and observations. She thought he was a true gentleman, like her father, someone who engendered trust and projected a calm resolve with his gentle, soothing Southern accent.

Larry found Betty Ann's freewheeling, open-book personality infectious and delightful. They bantered and teased each other in the way good friends of a different gender often do, sometimes allowing sexual innuendo and erotic banter to enter their conversations before retreating to safer territory with a dismissive touch on a wrist, the meaning of which was never clear to either of them.

It was Betty Ann who first surfaced the idea of romantic involvement between them. At the time they were discussing a study conducted by a storied university that revealed nearly a quarter of men admitted to having an extramarital affair and that their partners were most often close friends. Betty Ann tended to say what she thought, but it still shocked Larry when she asked the obvious question.

"You ever think about having an affair?" Betty Ann said between hearty sips of her scotch, as if inquiring about the weather.

"Never," Larry said definitively, a little defensively even, before adding, "but I try to avoid saying never, even on this topic. Stuff happens, you know, but I can't imagine it."

"So, you can't imagine any scenario that would make you stray from the straight and narrow," Betty Ann pressed, a bit tauntingly, recognizing an opportunity to tease a good friend.

"That's the thing about choices," he said, "you don't know the path you'll take until the choice is staring you down like a freight train."

"What if there were absolutely no chance, none whatsoever, you'd get caught?" Betty Ann asked, a bit coyly. "Would that make a difference?"

"Of course, it would," he said, "but then I'd still know. But if you throw in some memory-flushing pills, then sure, absolutely. The sad truth is men are born adulterers and the only thing stopping them is the worry that they'll be caught because most of them are awful liars and cowards to boot. Take that away, and all bets are off."

"I didn't know you were such a cynic," Betty Ann said.

"I'm not," Larry said, "but we're supposed to be in the truth business, and I'd say that is damn close to the truth, present company included."

The next day Larry and Betty Ann ran into each other after their morning meetings. They had lunch together out on the hotel's veranda overlooking the ocean. They ordered glasses of Pinot Grigio, a choice that seemed a perfect pairing with the distant muted sounds of crashing ocean waves. After their pleasant lunch, they made plans for dinner since it was the last night of the conference.

"Hey, we should celebrate tonight. Next week, it's back to the old grindstone," Larry offered.

"Are you buying?" Betty Ann said.

"Sure, we'll raid my generous expense account," he replied smiling.

"If you insist," she said, reaching across the table to touch Larry's hand, which was resting on the stem of his wineglass. "You are too kind, sir," she said in an exaggerated Southern accent, "too kind indeed."

Larry chuckled. "So, I'll see you at seven tonight," he said, standing up to leave.

"Goodness, you can't imagine how I'm looking forward to it," Betty Ann said, cuing up more of her overwrought Southern accent.

"All right, Ms. O'Hara," Larry said, smiling, "it's a date."

Although Betty Ann was thirty-five, she still looked youthful enough to have bartenders occasionally ask for her driver's license. But her youthful appearance and understated beauty took second rank to the strong, confident presence she exuded. It was a quality that drew the respect of her colleagues and made her a good leader. No colleague, male or female, questioned her authority or competence, even though she was younger than many of them by at least a decade.

However, Betty Ann also had a surprisingly relaxed, sometimes reckless side, especially in how she conducted her romantic life. On a solo trip to Paris a few years ago, she had met a kindred spirit, an architect from Sweden on holiday, and she had spent ten days with him before they said goodbye at the airport. It was an unspoken agreement between them when they walked away from each other at the Charles de Gaulle Airport that they would not stay in touch. The arrangement suited them both, although they had not explicitly said so.

While he waited for Betty Ann in the hotel lobby, Larry passed the time talking to colleagues and skimming the *New York Times* headlines to catch up on the day's news. He loved reading the crisp, clean language, and was reminded once again why the *Times* was still the best newspaper in the country. When he was in journalism school, he had had vague dreams of someday being a reporter for the *New York Times*, the *Washington Post*, or the *Chicago Tribune*, but he had only got as far as the *Atlanta Constitution* before cashing in whatever professional cache he had accumulated over the years to become the *Greenwood Clarion*'s publisher. Like Betty Ann, everyone was glad to have him home.

He was reading a long investigative piece about Wall Street avarice and criminality when he noticed Betty Ann walking across the lobby toward him. She was as stunningly beautiful as any woman he'd ever seen in his life. He dropped his arms into his lap, folding the paper like an accordion bellows and stared transfixed until Betty Ann stood directly in front of him.

"What's wrong with you, never seen a beautiful woman before?" Betty Ann said.

"Yes, of course," Larry stammered, truly struck speechless and perhaps a little frightened.

"Well, what do you say, then?" Betty Ann coaxed, holding her arms out and spinning around like a debutant.

"You look beautiful," he said, then added, "I mean really gorgeous!"

"Of course," she said, reverting to her Southern accent again. "I am always the belle of the ball."

Thinking back on the circumstances that led to their passionate tryst, Larry clearly recognized he had ignored every opportunity to walk away from disaster. But even now, it was hard to muster a sizable amount of remorse. Had it not been for the video, he was sure he and Betty Ann would have had an awkward laugh about their indiscretion the next day and vowed not to let it change their friendship, even though they both knew it would.

They had planned to have dinner in the hotel, but because they were both dressed for the ball—Larry was wearing his best sports jacket and a tasteful island shirt—it seemed a shame to waste the effort, so Larry called for reservations at the city's most expensive waterfront restaurant. And because it was a warm and sultry night, he asked for a table overlooking the ocean.

In hindsight, he was clearly responsible for setting into motion the perfect storm of circumstances that would blow up his life: dinner with a beautiful woman he really liked who was unfortunately not his wife; a seaside candlelit dinner under a cloudless, radiant sky full of stars; and a shimmering full moon that made the backlit ocean waves look iridescent. Once a bottle of wine and a couple of single malt scotches were added in, an inextinguishable fuse was lit, and all either one of them could do was pull up a chair and wait for the inevitable conflagration.

Larry and Betty Ann laughed at each other's jokes throughout dinner, although they did have a perfunctory discussion about the conference. Mainly, their conversation centered around their common literary and artistic interests. Larry said he was rereading all of Hemingway, and Betty Ann admitted she was trying to finally get through *Ulysses*. She told Larry about the two plays and a concert she'd recently seen in New York. She mentioned a ten-day New England biking trip she'd planned for the summer. Larry's life beyond work was less adventurous. He did offer that his family had a two-week vacation planned at their beach house in Duck.

After dinner, they walked along the boardwalk, and Betty Ann hooked her arm around Larry's until they decided to stroll on the beach. It was a calm, lovely evening, and Larry was reminded of similar beach walks he'd taken with Louisa May before life got complicated.

"What a beautiful evening," Larry offered. "I should do this more often."

"Oh, you mean take walks along the beach with the belle of the ball," Betty Ann said, smiling.

"No," he said, "but that's not such a bad idea now that you mention it. No, I mean take time to see the bigger picture and be present in the moment." Larry could tell his scotch buzz was now talking, but he continued, despite knowing full well he should leave it at that.

"That's something you help me do," he said, "slow down and just appreciate the stars in the sky and my good fortune. I don't know..."

"Are you unhappy?" she asked.

"No, I'm happy, most of the time," he said, "but sometimes I wish..."

"Wish what?" she probed.

"Nothing," Larry said, quickly retreating.

Walking back to the hotel, Betty Ann tried to get Larry to say what he wished for, but he deflected the question and asked her if she was ready for her panel discussion the next day, which was the last and usually poorly attended event of the conference.

On their way through the hotel lobby, Larry picked up two cut crystal glasses from behind the closed bar counter and suggested they have a nightcap by the hotel's elegant pool. Then, using his free hand, he reached inside his jacket and pulled out a sleek silver pocket flask with his initials on it. "My only concession to Southern dandy-hood," he confessed with a chuckle.

1 – Consequences

The pool was closed for swimming or even visiting, at least according to a sign posted on the gate, but they ignored the warning and clicked open the latch. Low-voltage garden lights illuminated their way around lushly planted islands of greenery. It all resembled a stage setting meant to give every collection of chairs a sense of privacy and isolation. They ultimately agreed on a comfortable-looking chaise daybed fitted with a clamshell umbrella and climbed under its cocoon-like structure as if they were two teenagers out on a lark. Larry poured his precious scotch into the heavy tumblers he had taken from the bar. Then they toasted each other.

"Here's to an interesting year," Betty Ann said, raising her glass.

"Yep," Larry said, "an interesting year."

It is hard to say who crossed the friends-only line first, but once crossed there was no going back. The magnetic pull of their long ignored mutual attraction was suddenly given free rein. On the security camera video that filmed their performance, it appeared as if the couple's clothes had suddenly caught fire, and they had determined the only way to save themselves was to remove them as quickly as possible.

Betty Ann won the race, and she helped Larry free himself of his encumbrances. Nearly thirty minutes of frantic lovemaking ensued. It was an impressive tour de force that Larry would have been proud of had it not been made publicly available like on-demand television. One of his best friends, Sam Johnson, a well-known local contractor, said as much one evening sitting on Larry's porch as they shared a beer and struggled to be heard over the cacophony of highway and rooftop air-conditioner noise.

"I don't know if this helps any," Sam said, "but I think you should be proud of that video, even if it's turning out to be a bit costly to you.

I mean, I got to say, that was some mighty fine work, mighty fine, my friend. Just saying is all."

"Thank you, Sam," Larry said, "and no, that's not very useful right now."

Since their clothes were already off and they had already broken pool rules about entering the area after hours—and for that matter, unwritten rules about nudity and public sex—Betty Ann suggested going for a swim in the pool. She was right about swimming not adding significantly to their list of poolside etiquette offenses, but leaving the daybed was a mistake. While they remained under the clamshell, plausible deniability was a potential escape route, but once outside its safe confines they might as well have been on a casting call for the rock musical *Hair*. It was also the moment in the video where most people in town who had the courage enough to admit they'd seen it exclaimed, "My God in heaven, that is Larry Fine with a woman who is not his wife, and they are as naked as the day they were born."

Most people stopped watching the video at this point for a variety of reasons, either disgust or embarrassment for Larry and his family, but mainly because the best parts were over.

Larry and Betty Ann saw each other only briefly the next day. After their early morning swim, they had collected themselves at the pool and returned to their separate rooms, a decision made with furtive, confused looks between them as they stood outside Betty Ann's hotel room door.

The next morning, Larry and Betty Ann hugged each other in the grand entrance hall and promised to keep in touch as they compared calendars to coordinate upcoming board committee meetings. They acted as if nothing had changed between them, but of course everything had changed and there was no way of putting that genie back in the bottle, even before the video surfaced.

Who was to blame for leaking the security footage of Larry and Betty Ann's poolside tryst is unclear, although the head of security was fired, and a thorough investigation was conducted into the incident. As for the identity of the person who first saw the video and shared it with the town's populace, that is a largely worthless part of the story and is, in the end, the absolute definition of water under the bridge.

What matters is that dozens of Larry's and Betty Ann's friends, neighbors, and family saw at least some parts of the video, and the consequences were immediate and real. Larry had to find a new place to live—at least for a time—and both Betty Ann's and Larry's family and friends were all less happy to have them home again.

The only positive side to the story is the vast resources Larry's family could muster to erase the video from the internet, beginning with the website that hosted it, something his family's legal team did with a vengeance. It took months to accomplish, but eventually even curious, tech-savvy teenagers could not find any active link to the video. That was encouraging, but even the best tech experts warned Larry's family that eliminating every copy of a video is nearly impossible once it's posted. In the meantime, Larry's lawyer stood ready to send out cease-and-desist letters at a moment's notice.

Six months on, the consequences of Larry's video performance had begun to fade, although Larry knew it would forever be part of his life's résumé, something brought up as a unique fact about him like once bungee-jumping off a bridge; however, starring in a short-lived sex tape would likely proceed it.

As it turned out, the people of Greenwood were more tolerant of his indiscretion than he expected, mainly because they found other indiscretions to gossip about. His job was secure because his family held the note on the *Clarion* building, but his father let him know that if a groundswell to remove him emerged, he'd be first in line to escort him out the door. "It's nothing personal, son," Marcus told Larry. "You'll always have the family's support, but business is business. I'm sure you understand."

The consequences at home were somewhat ameliorated at first by Larry's confession to Louisa May the week he returned from the conference. Clearly his contention that most men were terrible liars was prescient, a truth he realized straightaway when Louisa May asked if anything interesting had happened at the conference.

"Funny you should ask," he had said. "Something interesting did happen, although I suspect you'll have to expand your definition of interesting once I tell you."

In the weeks leading up to the video's release, rivers of tears had been shed as Louisa May and Larry worked through the pain, hurt, and guilt of the affair. He moved to one of the guest rooms, and he and Louisa May continued family life as normally as possible. But when she saw the video, Louisa May handed him a suitcase and asked him to be gone when she got back from the grocery store. That's when he moved to his shrinking investment property where he secretly hoped the unstoppable expansion of consumer culture would soon slice off the final portion of his remaining protective hill and take him and his little crappy house with it.

"So how are you doing?" his friend Sam said on one of his frequent visits. "You think Louisa May is ready to forgive you and let you come home?"

"I don't know, Sam," Larry said. "She's still pretty hurt, embarrassed, and pissed. And I don't blame her one bit."

"Yeah," Sam said, "your little dalliance ginned up some pretty significant consequences. But now that nobody can see your video, I suspect Louisa May will eventually begin to focus on the bigger picture and remember that you are still a decent husband and father."

"I hope she will see it that way eventually, but until that happens it looks like I'll be doing my penance here," Larry replied.

"I suspect that is true," Sam said, then added, more as an afterthought than anything else, "So, have you and Betty Ann been in touch?"

"Not for a while," Larry said, "and that's the shame of it . . . I really miss Betty Ann. We were really good friends."

"Well, I'd say that particular friendship train has permanently left the station, buddy," Sam said, "unless you enjoy living here."

"I know that, but I just—" Larry began to say before Sam cut him off.

"Hold it there," Sam said, "this is not a story you can make have a happy ending. There are consequences, plain and simple, like there is for every choice you make in life. Drink too many beers, you get a gut, and you ruin your liver. Don't plan for retirement, you end up living in a trailer park waiting for meals-on-wheels to bring your dinner. And in your case, cheating on your wife, even if Betty Ann was a good friend and you didn't mean for it happen, has its consequences; that is, sitting with me on the porch of this broken-down house instead of relaxing with Louisa May and your kids on that beautiful patio we built for you last summer."

"You're right," Larry said, "I guess I'm in a pretty deep hole."

"Yep, I am sorry to say you are," Sam said. He paused for a moment and then asked, "So, given the costs, you still think your little dalliance with Betty Ann was worth it?"

"Well, that's the thing," Larry said, "you'll have to ask me that question a few years from now, when and if Louisa May takes me back and all this is behind us. When I'm no longer defined by what I did. When people move on to other examples of human frailty and imperfection beyond mine. Ask me then and I might give you an honest answer."

They both allowed the question and Larry's equivocating answer to linger in the air without comment, although they knew full well what the truth was. Then they sat in silence and let the sound of the ugly, rooftop industrial machinery wash over them like rippling ocean waves as they stared at a distant vanishing point beyond the shopping mall and pondered what to say next.

2

Greenwood

ONE OF THE STORIES I TELL GREEN MANSION visitors as they crowd around a wall-size photograph of Lester Hamilton Green, my great-great-grandfather, is that when he brought the surrounding 1,500 acres of land here in 1852, he didn't know a railroad line would one day slice through the middle of it.

And he certainly didn't imagine—I usually say this in a dramatic way—that his name would be embedded in the future town's name or that he would one day enjoy listening to the sound of passing trains as he rocked on the veranda of his grand new home.

I tell visitors this story because it allows me to cast Lester as a high-flying risk taker, someone willing to put all his chips on the table and roll the dice based on instinct alone. It makes a better story than what is more likely the truth, that Lester always made sure the odds were in his favor before rolling any dice. In this case, Lester likely knew full well that the North Carolina Railroad Company planned to build its new eastbound line through his land. If luck played any part, it never had a starring role.

Still, I tell the story because it engages people and supports a powerfully held human belief—despite all the evidence against it—that the goddess of good fortune dispenses her favors randomly and equally. All you have to do is wait your turn. Perhaps it is such a conviction, as flawed as it is, that draws visitors to study one photograph in particular of Lester that hangs in the Green Mansion center entrance as if they were searching for a guardian angel hovering just above his head like lens flare.

In the photograph, Lester is standing beneath a welcome to Greenwood sign on the platform of the town's newly built train station holding an open pocket watch in the palm of his extended right hand. He is staring squarely at the camera with a humorless, even annoyed expression, as if the photographer had offended him in some way. I've often thought he looks like a bearded gray rock wearing a top hat.

The other photograph that tour groups like to study hangs on the opposite wall. Taken in 1870, it shows two buildings under construction behind the completed train station, one a general store and the other a livery stable. At the time, a good portion of the town's hundred or so early residents worked for Lester: some cutting heart pine, oak, hickory, and walnut planks at his sawmill; others laboring on his farm as blacksmiths and stable hands; and the rest working in his downtown businesses. I usually don't highlight these facts because it seems too Southern Gothic for one man to essentially own the entire town.

As director of the Green Mansion Foundation and the only direct descendant living on our ancestral property, I have tried to come to terms with our family's legends and its generational hypocrisies. Some of the more obviously fanciful ones, that Lester was a nineteenth-century billionaire, I try to set right. Other stories—that all the chandeliers were made in Murano, Italy—I only lightly correct by saying "perhaps" some were made there, even though most were made in Philadelphia or New York. These statements are not false per se. However, allowing them to stand creates a narrative of opulence our marketing manager says attracts paying visitors to our property. Still, my tolerance for structuring stories to our advantage is limited—or at least it used to be.

For example, I never allow anyone to say that Lester deserves a pass on his use of enslaved people because he was a mere participant in the moral and ethical standards of his day. I also don't allow anyone in my family to minimize our abundant White privilege, especially when a family member tells me our Ivy League educations and successful careers as prominent lawyers, bankers, or developers are due solely to our hard work and native intelligence.

Despite the ambivalence and occasional shame, I sometimes feel about my family's past and even my own success as a lawyer, I've made peace with both the good and the bad of my family's legacy. In fact, I've come to enjoy my small-pond celebrity here in Greenwood. Back in Washington, DC, where I lived until about ten years ago, my family history rarely rated a free cup of coffee unless one of our state senators or representatives was offering it. But here, my full family name, Hamilton Lester Green III, buys a measure of respect from the tour groups I lead, especially the local ones. And even though I ask them to address me by my nickname, which is Ham, most still insist on calling me Mr. Green.

How someone who spent a good portion of his life vowing never to live in his hometown ended up doing just that is one of those stories that begins with a phone call. In this case, it was a call from my straight-talking Aunt Betts who called my DC office to say she had been given the task of recruiting me to be the new Green Mansion Foundation director.

At the time, I let her know I was perfectly happy with both my employment and my newly renovated townhouse near the Eastern Market. Not one to mince words, she got immediately to the point. The foundation was in dire financial straits, and the board had determined I was the only one who could fix things. Without my help, she told me, a good portion of Lester's land would have to be sold to replenish the trust.

It was an unfair tactic, given that I worked for a nonprofit organization focused on preserving historic buildings and places. She knew I would feel duty bound to help, and so I agreed to make a few trips home to consult on possible solutions. That was the foot in the door Aunt Betts needed to convince me to take a short leave of absence to serve as temporary director. From there, the path was cleared for her to convince me I was somehow divinely chosen for the job and that I could, despite the opinion of one notable Southern writer, go home again.

Fortunately, Greenwood today is a more interesting town than the one I left years ago to attend boarding school in Connecticut. In those days, Greenwood was a town of about 25,000 residents, many of whom came to town on weekends to shop in the fifty or so turn-of-the-century buildings that still front its three principal thoroughfares, Main Street, Pine Street, and Green Street. It was a good town to grow up in, especially when your last name was Green since everyone seemed to know you or have some direct relationship to a family member. Such familiarity resulted in a deference I found both unremarkable and slightly annoying at times.

Then, as now, the area west of Greenwood's historic downtown core is zoned for service and retail business: grocery stores, auto body repair shops, HVAC companies, car dealerships, and the like. Most of the buildings on this side of town were constructed between the early 1920s and the 1970s, although big box retailers and strip malls have recently begun transforming the area. A new and unexpectedly attractive shopping center called Creek's Edge is the newest one, although it is nowhere near any creek.

Unfortunately, these new structures have replaced some of the area's more interesting buildings, including a former Studebaker dealership that still bore the defunct car maker's name, painted on its side wall in faded canary yellow. It is small consolation to local historians that a local photographer managed to snap a picture of the building and intact signage before it was reduced to rubble to make way for a new Ford dealership. A large sepia-toned print of the photograph now hangs in City Hall along with pictures of my relatives, a good number of whom are still involved in local politics.

Now, as then, the affluent residents live on the east side of town on land that once belonged to Lester. The homes, stately Queen Anne, Romanesque Revival, and Second Empire for the most part, are situated on their original one-to-two-acre plots of land. Most were built between 1900 and 1915 for the town's professional class of doctors, lawyers, and such and even a few families that managed to hold on to their generational wealth after the Civil War.

Green Mansion, a Georgian and Neoclassical gem recognized in the National Register of Historic Places, is considered part of this eastside neighborhood, although the mansion itself is more than a mile from the closest estate house. Still, for those living here, which at one time included me, Lester's remaining eight hundred acres are a convenient, private refuge, especially for those who can claim our grounds as part of their own impressively landscaped backyards.

On the north side, the residents are mostly working and middle class, although an increasing number of homes are being renovated by an influx of well-educated young people who favor more bedrooms and storage space than reasonably necessary. The south side is still predominantly populated by people of color, although that was not the term people used when I was growing up. But even this neighborhood is changing as it welcomes more tax and home price refugees from the north side who must move to find a home they can afford.

Ten years after my reluctant return, I cherish my life here with Cara Ann McCabe, my wife, and our two dogs, Max and Miller. Our two children, Candice and Katherine, one still in law school and the other working for a nonprofit focused on stopping gender-based violence around the world, live in DC. They visit us on occasion, although they never stay long when they do.

Our own house is a large four-square farmhouse that my grandfather, Samuel P. Green, built right before the turn of the twentieth century for the last sharecropping family to work our land. The house has a wide porch that hugs the meticulously restored clapboard siding that our maintenance staff keeps in pristine condition. It is where Cara and I sit most evenings to have a glass of wine and talk about the day's events. At night, the old house creaks and cracks and moans like an elderly person getting up to find the TV remote, and when it rains the tin roof clatters and pings and pongs like we're being attacked by a SWAT team. I enjoy these sounds as much as I imagine my great-great-grandfather enjoyed hearing the mournful, dissipating sounds made by a train's steam whistle as it whipped past the newly built Greenwood Station late at night.

2 – Greenwood

It's a life far away from the one Cara and I left behind in DC. Before settling into her life here, Cara worked as a legislative assistant on Capitol Hill for a powerful, liberal senator from Massachusetts. She loved her job and understandably found it difficult to give up the adrenaline rush she got from meeting impossible deadlines and serving alongside a true Washington power broker. In fact, the withdrawal process took nearly two years, a time we spent living separately until she was ready to leave, and then only because her boss retired.

Those years of living separate lives did impose a great difficulty on our marriage and from what I have since come to understand, the senator retired just in time. It's a topic we don't bother to discuss or even think about these days because it's a waste of energy and completely irrelevant to our lives now.

As it is, Cara luxuriates in her new life. She gets up every morning at 6:30 A.M. and walks our dogs, wearing only her well-used bathrobe and a broken-down pair of Crocs. I tell her she looks like a shabby version of Queen Elizabeth exercising her pack of corgis on the grounds of Windsor Castle. It's an ongoing joke that always gets a smile.

Afterward, Cara drives the four miles to downtown Greenwood to open her home furnishings and gift shop called The Happy Clam. It's a business that occupies a former department store, and her success has sparked a revival of downtown. An excellent restaurant recently opened next door in the menswear store where my father bought his suits and my mother picked out my wardrobe for boarding school.

Cara is exceedingly proud of what she's accomplished here. She's president and founder of the Greenwood Retail Association, and she has used her Capitol Hill political savvy to get a change-resistant city government to support her vision of making downtown a destination at least equal to Green Mansion. She tells me she is happy to be here and thanks me quite often for forcing her hand to move here, as if that were even possible.

My own office is nearly a mile away in the Green Mansion Visitors' Center. It's a state-of-the-art facility with a large auditorium and a sizable museum with interpretative and interactive displays designed by a former Smithsonian curator. The center has a pleasant café that overlooks a manicured patch of pathways defined by boxwoods and seasonal swatches of stunningly beautiful red, white, and pink roses. It's a first-rate facility, and clearly the architect hired by our board spared no expense on materials to create it. This includes solid, two-inch thick walnut doors, gleaming, stately brass hardware, and restrooms so sumptuous and comforting I look forward to using them.

Unfortunately, my family's elusive pot of gold wasn't there to pay for all the expensive palace-like elegance, and the resulting cash flow shortage is part of what got the former director sacked and precipitated Aunt Betts's full court press recruiting mission to hire me so that I could somehow save the day.

Be that as it may, I usually walk the distance to my office on a pea gravel pathway through gardens that always seem to have something blooming in them: banks of roses beginning in May; viburnum, tulips, hollyhock, zinnia, and dahlia in the spring; allium, gladiolus, ginger, cosmos, and foxglove in the summer; chrysanthemum, cockscomb, iris, and sunflowers in the fall. As I walk, I focus on each footfall and try to be as mindful as possible, but I'm often distracted by the crunching, spitting sound made by the gravel, a sound not unlike walking on a bed of breakfast cereal.

Some days, if my mindfulness practice fails me, I pretend I'm walking with Cara in the Tuileries Gardens. It's a place made for observing native Parisians from a cast-iron park bench as they stroll past conversing with one another, the young women often pushing elegant prams. Cara likes to eavesdrop on the fast-paced conversations, exchanges so full of urban colloquial expressions that even Cara, who is fluent in French, hardly understands a word of it.

In the event of rain, I drive to work in a cream-colored enclosed golf cart with impressive decals on the front and back that say Greenwood Mansion Trust, something the profligate former director was criticized for buying. However, on inclement days I have to admire his impeccable foresight.

For my part, I have made the trust a smooth-running and solvent entity, but those first years were like being a firefighter on call twenty-four hours a day. I even propped up the foundation for a time with a loan guaranteed by the value of my DC townhouse. At the time I appealed to anyone who might have cash, an approach that meant I concentrated my efforts on the wealthy and well-connected philanthropists I knew from my time in Washington.

At home, I appealed directly to the Greenwood community through our local newspaper, the *Greenwood Clarion*, by convincing the publisher, Larry Fine, a longtime friend of the family, to run a series of articles about Green Mansion and its cultural and financial significance to the community. Larry personally wrote the articles, focusing principally on the many reasons to *support* the trust rather than *save* it, a semantic dance we felt necessary given the hard reality that most people find it difficult to care about the financial problems of the well-to-do. It's not something I blame them for.

Eventually, a wealthy entrepreneur who was born in Greenwood but now lived in Charlotte, fully funded the trust and really did, in fact, save the day. Despite this fortunate turn of events, I still spend a good bit of my time dialing for dollars in one way or another, so that managing the grounds and administrative staff and conducting tours a few hours each week makes for a busy but fulfilling work schedule.

Still, the foundation's workload does not prevent me from occasionally driving downtown to see Cara at her shop, a visit that surprises and delights her. If she gets busy with her customers, I say goodbye and walk down the street to see Dixie Leigh McBride, owner of Dixie's Diner on Main Street. Dixie is someone I count on to serve up her opinion on any topic, something she continues to do while sliding a stained and chipped mug of coffee in my direction, always with a single-ply napkin folded neatly underneath the saucer.

We chat mainly about local news, most of which is not in Larry's paper. And if the timing works out, Cara might join me for lunch, a simple, unremarkable activity that can unleash a flood of emotions that leaves me feeling grateful and perhaps a little sad. Gratitude on the one hand for the sweetness of my life and its meaningful, deep connections, and on the other hand, loss, regret, and sadness for abandoning the warm embrace of my family and our community for all these years.

A few years ago, either as an act of redemption, or perhaps existential angst, I took it upon myself to write a comprehensive history of Greenwood and Green Mansion. Although we sell reprints of Lester's 1895 biography, his formal, stuffy prose is hard to decipher. It's mainly a paperweight that few, except for die-hard members of the Daughters of the American Revolution, would ever admit to reading. Even so, we sell a fair number of copies in our gift shop along with high-profit tchotchkes, such as branded T-shirts, hats, key chains, umbrellas, and water bottles, all of which help keep the doors open and the gardens trimmed and watered.

2 – Greenwood

The book I eventually published created quite a stir in the community, but not for the reasons I had first anticipated. My intention at the outset was to strip away the mythology of Lester's larger-than-life persona to uncover who he really was other than a towering intellect who discovered his prodigious intellectual abilities at an exceptionally young age. In fact, he claims in his book that he served as his common school's substitute instructor when his regular teacher was sick or otherwise unavailable.

According to Lester's accounting, a wealthy indigo plantation owner by the name of Ezra Lucas first recognized his native intelligence during a brief conversation they had in the spring of 1839 on the steps of the Charleston Library Society building, even then one of the nation's oldest lending libraries.

As the story goes, Lester, who was fifteen at the time, had traveled to Charleston from his family's farm about fifteen miles northwest of Charleston to help his father gather up a few farming and household supplies. The library must have been magnetic to someone like Lester, who had an apparently insatiable appetite for books and knowledge. Perhaps he thought he could stand near the King Street building and somehow absorb the knowledge inside by proximity alone.

Why Ezra came to the library that day is unknown (perhaps Lester did have a guardian angel). Nevertheless, the connection Lester and Ezra made that day was a powerful one.

Lester says that Ezra escorted him back to his father, who was relaxing from his labors in a popular pub, and introduced himself, telling Lester's father how impressed he was with Lester's precocious intellect.

It was a connection that eventually led to Lucas offering Lester a job on his plantation. Apparently, my great-great-grandfather was also a horse whisperer of exceptional talent. Lester does not dwell on what his family thought about his job on the Lucas plantation, but he does say his parents were extremely proud of him when he graduated, first from the College of Charleston and later William & Mary Law School, all on Ezra's dime. Green Mansion's ornate, skylighted library with its thousands of beautifully bound leather books and its polished walnut tables and book stands is a testament to Lester's love of libraries. Most visitors claim it is their favorite room in the mansion.

According to an 1890 inventory of his books, Lester's library contained nearly 15,000 volumes that covered a full range of topics, including mathematics, science, history, and an impressive collection of the most celebrated novelists and poets of his day, including Herman Melville, Walt Whitman, and Henry David Thoreau. Surprisingly, the inventory also lists a copy of *Uncle Tom's Cabin* by Harriet Beecher Stowe.

As for Green Mansion, Lester notes construction began in 1856 when he was thirty-two years old and that the house was finished right before Confederate General Beauregard fired on Fort Sumter in April of 1861. Despite the war, Lester married one of Ezra's nieces, Maribelle Della Parsons, in June of that year. He and his new bride soon moved to his home in the heart of what was then a veritable wilderness compared with Charleston, which was then, as it is now, one of the most fashionable, elegant cities in the nation. Lester does not explain why he didn't fight on the front lines with his Confederate comrades, mentioning only that he was a local militia member and that he supplied basic food and material support to the troops.

But here is where I have always questioned Lester's story and his motives. Yes, it makes business sense to invest in property even if that investment is hundreds of miles from your hometown, and yes, marrying into a wealthy family was a smart choice for an ambitious man like Lester. But the idea that he would take his bride to an elegant but remote mansion far from his friends and the valuable connections he'd made over the years never made sense to me.

That is, until I found a cache of letters from a woman named Hattie McBride carefully stuffed behind a row of law books in his library, historical documents that generations of Greens, and even our conservators, missed finding for more than one hundred years.

Of course, the fact that Lester had a secret life is not surprising: most ambitious and powerful men hold secrets of one kind or another, and these hidden shames often involve couplings between men and women of all persuasions. Lester's shame or delight was Hattie, a lover of long standing for whom he clearly cared deeply, judging by the nearly ten years of correspondence I found.

Like many such liaisons, then and now, this affair was complicated by a pregnancy that produced a son, whose name was Hamilton McBride. He would have been about nine years old in 1870 when the first surviving letter was written. In that letter, Hattie responds in great detail to Lester's questions about her life in Philadelphia where she and her young son moved after the war. It must have been satisfying for Lester to learn that Hamilton was just as precociously smart as he had been at a young age with an all-consuming love of books, libraries, and reading.

The one detail that keeps this from being just another story of a hidden affair is this one complicating factor. Hattie was not a disgraced member of the Charleston plantation aristocracy. Nor was she a ribald, fun-loving peasant woman whose company Lester enjoyed a little too much, someone forced to flee Charleston to escape the shame of an out-of-wedlock child. No, as it turned out, Hattie

McBride was the Lucas family's favorite nanny, an enslaved young girl who lived in the Lucas family attic, someone Lester professed to love with his "full and tender heart."

By the time Cara got home on the day I found the letters, I had already read them numerous times and had taken pages of notes. It was all logical activity, but I still felt as if I'd found a ticking time bomb that needed dismantling before it blew up in my face. I'm sure I was wild-eyed when Cara walked into my office after draping her jacket over an empty kitchen chair. She poured herself a generous glass of wine.

"Are you OK?" she asked, leaning against a doorframe. "You look rattled. Anything wrong?"

"You might say that" I replied, "but to tell the truth, I can't say which it is: whether everything is wrong, or that finally, everything is right. It's something I definitely need your opinion on."

I could see Cara formulating her reply, so I put my hand up signaling her to hold that thought. "Yea, I know," I said, gently, "I'll meet you on the porch, and I'd advise you to bring the rest of that bottle of wine with you."

I spent the next half hour telling Cara about the letters I'd found. My explanation lasted long enough for the sun to slip lazily below the distant horizon and for the crickets and cicadas to begin their nightly racket.

Cara mainly listened like a trained therapist, but I could see her Capitol Hill strategic wheels turning, reacting to every question or conclusion I had written down on my yellow legal pad. On the last page, I had written what I thought was an essential set of questions: how to determine the letter's authenticity, what would be a reasonable public response, and who to tell first, board members or immediate family. As the last entry I had written three words, all in capital letters: TELL NO ONE. I thought Cara would advise scratching that one out immediately, except she didn't.

"First, this is a story you have to get in front of," Cara said when I finally let her speak and her crisis management experience emerged. "The last thing you want is for this story to get out before you find out if it's true. Once out, true or not, it never goes away. And if it is true, then the foundation will have to embrace it, own it, as the folks at Monticello did when they finally embraced Thomas Jefferson's relationship with Sally Hemings, although it took DNA evidence and nearly two hundred years of accusations to bring entrenched interests around. Now, there's even a Sally Hemings descendants society, so it can be handled."

I nodded agreement because Cara was on a roll.

"So, here's what I'd do if I were in your position," she said, confirming once again why she had been so good at her job.

"First, verify that this story is true," she said. "I have a friend who is an Ancestry.com wizard. I can have her come by, set up your account, and give you some tips on how to search. You are, after all, working on a book about your family so there's nothing underhanded about that. Once you confirm or debunk the basic facts of Hattie McBride's story, you should alert the board because you don't want to be accused of sitting on the story if this gets out."

"I can see why the senator didn't want you to leave," I said when she took a break. "You're really good at this."

"I had to be," she replied smiling. "Senator Maddox was hard to keep on the straight and narrow, although he was better than most and I was never called on to directly lie, mostly just spin the facts in the right direction."

I was going to say that the word "spin" sounded a lot like lying to me but thought better of it as I was in no position to be sanctimonious in the face of my own crisis. If the story about Hattie McBride was true, which I thought it was, then I'd be the spinner in chief as our foundation pushed a narrative focused on Lester's fondness—even love—for Hattie; a story that tried to minimize the fact that Hattie was an enslaved woman and nowhere near a free agent in the world, someone who was unable to make her own decisions about where she lived and whom she invited to her bed. I understood my own hypocrisy all too well and felt bad about it, but I soothed the guilt by convincing myself that a full accounting of Hattie and Lester's relationship would put everything in a more balanced and reasonable light, aka spin.

Now three years since making it public, Hattie McBride's story is more popular than Lester Green's story. In fact, Hattie McBride's story is an asset to the foundation. She is revered for her courage and accomplishments and as a tough, determined woman who left the Lucas plantation in 1865 with her five-year-old son and built a new life for herself in Philadelphia. Someone who would not allow the shackles of her past to keep her from getting a college degree and becoming a teacher in a great northern city. Her son, Lester's son, graduated from college and did well as an investor and writer in New York City.

The other side benefit of publishing *The Courage of Hattie McBride* is that people actually take time to read our book because it's more than a history book. I often get complimentary emails from readers, part of the word-of-mouth support that has made the book a local bestseller. Once in a while, someone will even suggest that Hattie's story would make a good movie, something

I don't encourage. It's a small-pond story, I tell them, and one that Hollywood is not interested in. This is likely true, but to tell the truth I am happy for Hattie's story to remain a local one, an outcome that wasn't guaranteed once I began digging through my family's history to confirm the letter's authenticity.

Cara was, of course, right about getting ahead of the story. Once I told our board about what I'd found, the story leaked as we knew it would. The press and many citizens excoriated Lester for his abuse of an enslaved young woman, barely twenty years old when their relationship began. I didn't push back from the onslaught of criticism or argue that Lester's affection for Hattie in any way absolved him from the charge of exploitation.

Still, I controlled the piling on by alternately condemning my ancestor's action while arguing, tepidly but effectively, that Lester and Hattie had—despite the unequal power that Lester welded—a sincere love for each other based on the letters and other documents I uncovered. It was fortunate that when Hattie died in 1918 one of her relatives had the foresight to keep Lester's letters.

Throughout the book-writing process, I often wondered about how our community might react to the dynamics of race in Lester and Hattie's relationship. If Hattie had been White and a member of the ruling class, or even a farmer's daughter, and their indiscretion produced a son, would the community's reaction have been the same? It's an ugly question, the answer to which is obscured by both the White privilege and overt racism that our town is still trying to grapple with.

Lester did seem to recognize the untenable position he and Hattie found themselves in and that he could do nothing to change the trajectory of their relationship despite his wealth and status. In a letter dated June 4, 1878, Lester points to these immutable restraints and expresses regret that he and Hattie would always be forced to live separate, distant lives.

"Of all I have accomplished in my tenure upon this earth and the victories and rewards that life has bestowed upon me," Lester wrote to Hattie when he was nearly sixty-four years old, "I have but one regret, and it is the unredeemable disappointment of not being able to share both the joy and sorrow of life's journey with you and our son Hamilton. It is one of the few regrets I have in a life that has always treated me so kindly and with such good fortune I can scarcely imagine the goodness of the architect who has bestowed on me these many blessings."

Reading Lester's letters to Hattie did give me some sympathy for their situation, despite the impenetrable layers of assumption that prevented true understanding. Lester did have a deeply felt affection for Hattie—notwithstanding the disturbing power dynamics—and I do appreciate the difficulty of living with forbidden emotions. Maribelle, Lester's wife, dutifully produced a brood of heirs for Lester—five children, three boys and two girls—and Lester loved and provided well for his family. Yet, I suspect Maribelle was more a domestic decoration for his life, someone who knew how to throw a party and charm his guests with her refined manners.

Researching Hattie's book also forced me to give at least some credence to a story that I had heard repeated numerous times by family members: that Lester quietly released his enslaved workers beginning in 1863 and helped them escape north with cash in one pocket and papers for formerly enslaved people in the other. The reason this story is hard to pin down with historical records is because Lester's contemporaries might not have appreciated his enthusiastic support of Lincoln's 1863 Emancipation Proclamation. Had they known, his neighbors might have burned down his house and run him out of town on a rail.

After all, the end of the war was still nearly two years away and most landed gentry were not ready to declare the war a lost cause. I can only offer theories to explain how he might have gotten away with such an emancipation plot; perhaps he explained the missing workers by saying they were dead and that he was temporarily replacing them with paid workers. I simply don't know. In his biography, Lester does not address the issue, although he expresses remorse for his participation in the evil of slavery and says he was overjoyed to see it end.

Writing the book took two years and exposed our family and me personally to abuse and praise in equal measure. Some locals wanted to excuse Lester's relationship with Hattie as an unfortunate reality of the "times" and, as awful as it was, allowed that slavery was just a required part of the South's commercial model.

Others were more radical in their response. These locals claimed the only true cathartic response for our family and the town must include demolishing Green Mansion and changing the name of our town. I tried to thread the needle between the two extremes by placing Hattie at the center of the book's narrative and concentrating on her resiliency in the face of incredible hardship.

Creating such a comprehensive narrative meant I had to spend a good deal of time in Philadelphia's West End neighborhood where Hattie moved after leaving Charleston. Unfortunately, little of her physical presence survived the slash-and-burn urban development policies of the 1960s.

I was able to channel Hattie while strolling in Clark Park, a public space established during the years she lived there. I imagined Hattie as a tough and determined figure, walking with Hamilton among the newly planted trees, perhaps having a picnic with my distant relation underneath the sparse shade of a still maturing oak tree.

I thought how it might please her to know her old neighborhood is a bastion of higher education: both the University of Pennsylvania and Drexel University are nearby. Education was the escape route she sought passionately for herself and her son. It is at least worth saying, although it's not something that brings much pride, that Lester's escape from his own life of hardship was also education, but in his case, his deliverance was financed and supported by the work of enslaved people, Hattie McBride included.

The only physical evidence of Hattie was a placard I stumbled across in her old neighborhood that described the accomplishments of those who lived in the now bulldozed townhouses. The placard listed musicians, authors, politicians, and other notable persons, including one Hamilton Lester McBride, who according to the historical marker was a "successful businessman, investor, and the author of books on African American entrepreneurship."

I didn't know how to feel about seeing the name and accomplishments of a direct relative on a placard in this neighborhood, a relation that Lester Green's own family and descendants would have rejected outright had they known about him even twenty-five years ago, much less a hundred years ago.

As it is, people in town have absorbed the story of Hattie and Lester into our town's historical record and added their own spins to the truth I laid out in my book. Most of what I hear falls somewhere between mild curiosity and thinly veiled racism. Still, in general, everyone I talk to seems nonplussed and is more interested in hearing the details of what I chose to leave out of the book. I resist answering these questions because there are more interesting things to talk about in such a closely connected town.

For now, I'm just happy to be on the other side of Hattie's story and living my life again, walking to work through fabulous gardens, using the sumptuous visitors' center restrooms, watching the sunset with Cara from our porch, and accepting a free cup of coffee once in a while from Dixie McBride who has her own unique perspective on Hattie's story.

"So, you think Hattie and I might be related somehow?" Dixie asked recently as she sloshed another cup of coffee across her counter in my direction.

"I don't think so, Dixie. Hattie just adopted that name, McBride, to distance herself from her enslaved past. But who knows, you might be," I said.

"I think I'd like that," she replied. "It seems to me Hattie had real spunk, someone who didn't let anyone tell her what to do. In fact, I'd be proud to have a little of Hattie's blood in my veins."

"I suspect you would," I replied, "and if you want to spread that gossip around, I'd be glad to back you up. That'd really give people something to talk about."

"It's just what this town needs, don't you think? Something else to be outraged about besides taxes and the latest big box retail store to move in. Nothing like a forbidden love affair to liven things up."

"You might be an outlier on that," I said, reminding Dixie of the general conservatism of the people she served coffee and breakfast to every morning.

"I don't think so," she said. "People have to get over themselves. My God, it's a damn short trip, and taking time to worry about who loves whom and why they do. Well, that's one hundred percent stupid.

I think your great-great-grandfather and Hattie knew that and just said to hell with it. I mean, yes, the relationship was *wrong*—" (She made air quotes.) "—because he was married, and yes, it was absolutely wrong that Hattie was owned by another human, and yes, your great-great-grandfather did abuse his power over her no matter how you slice it. But from what I can tell from reading your book, they did love each other on some level, and it's just a shame that she wasn't allowed to live in Green Mansion with him as husband and wife, but that's life, you don't always get what you want. Still, I have to respect them both for the love they seemed to share, but that's just me, I might be an outlier on this as well."

"That's highly likely," I said, "but I think more people share your opinion than might admit it," thinking all of a sudden that I'd done too good of a spin job. Still, I'd have to agree with Dixie. Lester did care for Hattie more than his wife, Maribelle. And although I never found any evidence, I want to believe that Lester and Hattie did see each other again. Perhaps Lester even met his son at some point. Arranging such a meeting would have been easy given his wealth and influence.

"So," I asked Dixie, who seemed to be in a philosophical mood, "do you think Hattie is a victim or a hero in my story?"

"That's a question above my status as a coffee slinger and restaurant owner," she answered, "but, if you're interested, I'd say we're all victims, to a greater or lesser degree, of our collective hypocrisies, prejudices, racism, fears, and jealousies—all that divisive hatred we feel for other classes, neighborhoods, communities, cities, regions, and countries, and mostly directed toward people we don't know a damn thing about."

"That's a pretty profound assessment for a coffee slinger," I commented.

"Well, I spend my days with all kinds of people," Dixie continued, "and I hear a lot of things, some of it batshit crazy and some of it as reasoned and truthful as any college professor might say. But for my money, the only thing that cuts across it all—and this isn't some sentimental claptrap I'm giving you—is the love between two people. It's that human connection that ultimately matters, and it's about the only thing that's ever going to change the human condition for the better."

"You're a smart woman," I said.

"Yeah?"

"I mean it. In fact, I'd say you might be the second smartest woman in town," I said, mischievously. "Sorry, but that honor must by rights go to Cara, as I'm sure you understand."

"That's fine, I'll take it," Dixie said, moving away from the lunch counter and wiping the spot in front of her with a stained kitchen towel.

"I'll tell her the next time she joins you for lunch," she said.

"You do that for me, and I'll surely owe you one."

"I know you will," she replied, "and don't think I won't collect on it either. I'm not ever one to let a debt go unpaid or the truth go unsaid."

Dixie turned and headed back to the kitchen. I left a few extra dollars on the counter and walked back up the street to wave to Cara through her storefront window before I got in my car to drive back to Green Mansion. For the first time in a long time, I felt more hopeful and not just about the foundation's survival.

3

Dumbo Gets His Day

JIMMY JOHNSON WAS BORN WITH EXCEPTIONALLY large ears. Certainly not as ridiculously large as Dumbo, the cartoon character, but large enough to make him the butt of elephant ear jokes until his head size caught up with his ears.

It didn't help that his mother, Edna Joyce Johnson, insisted on her son having a buzz cut that left only a quarter inch of stubble on his head, a grooming decision that only emphasized his ears and made his head look like a kitchen well-used scrub brush. In fairness to Jimmy's mother, a buzz cut seemed a practical choice because it was easier for his mother to check for ticks and chiggers when Jimmy returned from the hunting expeditions he went on with his cousins in the nearby woods. They hardly ever killed any living creatures and instead mercilessly disintegrated empty glass beer bottles and tin cans with their 410 shotguns and the single-shot twenty-two-caliber rifle that they took care to line up on an old rotting fence.

3 – Dumbo Gets His Day

Once Jimmy got to junior high school his mother encouraged him to grow his hair to a more reasonable length because she worried that his ears—which were by then more proportional to his head—might still be a social liability. Unfortunately, even a thick head of hair could not protect him from the abuse still meted out by class bullies who continued to call him Dumbo even after he got a full scholarship to Brown University.

One might be tempted to put a feel-good spin on Jimmy's academic achievements and to hold up his success against the abuse he endured as some kind of karmic counterbalance or even as a good example of how one can leave adolescent trauma behind, a last-laugh narrative where good triumphs over evil. And while all that is true enough, it is not the whole story because the origins of Jimmy's extraordinary intelligence and his successful life that followed are inextricably linked to the place where Jimmy sought refuge from his abusers, the Greenwood Public Library.

Jimmy's affinity for the library began when he was a child. It was a place his mother took him nearly every Saturday afternoon. He vividly remembers how he sat transfixed on a child-themed rug—friendly-looking tigers and bears in a jungle setting—listening to Mrs. Hartnett, the librarian with a dramatic arts degree, read books to the gathered children with a theatrical flourish that sometimes frightened him.

And although he devoured fiction books by the dozens from an early age—some way beyond his years—he really loved science fiction books with shapeshifting characters who could transform themselves into anything they pleased. These fantastical narratives surely intrigued and transported Jimmy, but what really fired his imagination was the real or imagined science, math, and technological wonders that underpinned many of the storylines. It was this keystone interest that eventually led to his full scholarship to Brown.

By the time Jimmy entered his junior year in high school, he had, for the most part, moved past the debilitating effects of his early traumatic experiences. Even his teachers saw the change and noted in his report cards they believed Jimmy was finally "coming out of his shell." To his teachers this emergence was manifested in how much Jimmy interacted with his classmates, and specifically how he seemed less embarrassed to always know the answer to just about every question raised in class.

To his mother, her son's emergence from his shell was directly attributable to Jimmy's discovery of girls and one girl in particular, Charlene Ravenport, an outgoing, smart, well-liked class beauty who wore her thick glasses like a badge of honor and refused all entreaties to improve her social status by getting contact lenses.

Unlike Jimmy, Charlene was self-assured and liked being the center of attention. She was approachable and kind, and had Jimmy ever worked up the nerve to talk to her, she would have made his day. Instead, he admired her like one views a work of art in a museum; beautiful, untouchable, unattainable, and best enjoyed from a proper distance.

Then, one day at the end of a school assembly the school's principal, Mr. Watson, announced that the Panther Booster Club would sponsor a fundraising dance in two months' time. A collective groan rose from the room. Mr. Watson immediately moved to regain control.

"I understand your skepticism," he said, "but hear me out. This will be an event unlike any other, and I guarantee by the end of the night everyone in this room will be dancing."

The principal then outlined the big fundraising idea, something he described as a spring dance with its historical roots in dime-a-dance,

Depression-era dance halls. Except in this modern version, participating students (both male and female) would charge a small fee for the privilege of dancing with them with the proceeds going to the booster club. He decided against offering more historical context to the restless, uninterested teenagers and instead waited out another round of chatter and laughter before continuing.

"I know this is different, but please give it a chance," he said in a serious tone that stopped just short of pleading. "Besides, it's a great way to show school spirit, and you never know, you might just make some new friends." More groans erupted, but Mr. Watson let it go and explained the rules of selling dances to raise money and how the event would be structured to allow everyone to participate.

The next day, the principal's assistant created a half-dozen poster board sign-up sheets and taped them to an empty wall outside Mr. Watson's office. When he left for lunch, Mr. Watson noted with concern that no one had signed up for the dance. But when he returned, he was heartened to see a neatly written name, Charlene Ravenport, floating between the poster's carefully drawn lines underneath the heading "Fundraiser Participant." No one had yet signed up to buy a dance from her, but Mr. Watson was still grateful and encouraged by Charlene's bravery to sign up first.

Over the next few days, more students followed Charlene's example, and not just girls from the cheerleading squad and other always enthusiastic students. There was also a sizable showing of sought-after male students, mostly sports heroes, and even a few members of a popular student rock band. Within a few days, dozens of other students had followed Charlene's lead. Suddenly, everyone seemed willing to risk teenage humiliation in service to school spirit.

When Jimmy saw Charlene's name on the dance roster, he was filled with excitement, a feeling that was quickly overshadowed by anxiety when it occurred to him that he'd never danced in his life, not even when alone in his room. Undaunted, he wrote his name next to Charlene's in one of the ten remaining spots allotted to Charlene. Years later, after he had graduated from Brown in mathematics and was a self-assured and highly paid adult, James (formerly Jimmy) still marveled at his chutzpah—a word he was not even vaguely familiar with at the time.

Finding someone to teach him to dance wasn't as difficult as he'd first thought. Jimmy knew a small coterie of kindhearted girls who surely would help, but he didn't want to ask because touching them, even as a dance partner, somehow crossed a line he couldn't name. Then he found the obvious choice, Amanda Baker, his sister Jane's best friend, who practically lived with the family. She was on the cheerleading squad, which meant she absolutely knew how to dance.

"So, Amanda," Jimmy said, when he found her rummaging in the family's refrigerator the day after he'd signed up for the dance, "can I talk to you about something?"

"Sure," she said, closing the refrigerator door with her hip while balancing a jar of strawberry jam in the palm of one hand and a container of peanut butter in the other.

"I don't know how to ask you this other than to just say it," he said, surprised at his own directness, "but could you teach me to dance so I can go to the Panther fundraiser?"

To his surprise, Amanda immediately agreed to help for several reasons, not the least of which was her conviction that every Panther cheerleader had the responsibility to share the joy of movement, and, if she were honest, she thought Jimmy was cute, although still not a suitable alternative to quarterbacks.

"I'd love to do that, Jimmy," she said. "I believe everyone has the gift of dance in them. All you need to do is follow your body. It knows what to do."

Clearly, Amanda took this approach to heart, judging from her athletic sideline performances, which were filled with precisely executed somersaults, backflips, and handstands that she often transitioned into upside-down splits that formed a perfect letter T. Such acrobatics had been known to attract quite a crowd at major sporting events, and more than a few onlookers worried out loud that her strenuous, unnatural activity might somehow affect her childbearing capability later in life.

After she finished her sandwich, she took Jimmy's hand, which thrilled him more than he expected, and pulled him to the center of the family room, and asked Jimmy to help her move a coffee table stacked with magazines and books. "No time like the present," she said. Thus began Jimmy's dancing lessons.

It took a few weeks to make significant progress because lessons had to be squeezed in among homework, after-school activities, and those slender slices of time when no one was around to gawk or encourage him; both forms of attention he hated equally. Amanda was a patient teacher as she demonstrated each classic dance step: ball change, chaîné turns, swing, salsa, and unfettered freeform (her favorite). She showed Jimmy how to use these and other steps to feel relaxed and in charge of his body, something Jimmy wanted to learn because his greatest fear was looking like he was having a seizure on the dance floor.

"You're doing great, Jimmy," Amanda said one afternoon. "If you ask me, I'd say you're a natural dancer who will be the beau of the ball, so to speak." Amanda was known for her easy distribution of compliments, a habit that Jimmy had noticed about enthusiastic people.

Every few days Jimmy stopped by the principal's office to see if others had signed up to dance with Charlene. He noted she had eight customers, six boys and two girls, which was nearly her dance quota for the event. It was Mr. Watson's idea to limit the number of dance partners any one participant was allowed to accept. He shuddered thinking about the train wreck of hurt feelings and recriminations that would ensue if less popular students had empty dance cards while the most popular students had long wait lists. He knew this would reflect poorly on his leadership.

A few days before the dance, referred to officially as "A Night Out for Panther Pride," Jimmy's sister Jane said she was glad he was going to the fundraiser. She even offered to help him pick out an outfit.

"Amanda's been telling me about your dance lessons," Jane said before offering a rare sisterly compliment, "and she says you're not bad. I'm proud of you. Who knows, maybe Charlene will be impressed enough to go out with you." Jimmy blushed at the thought and mumbled out a "thank you," thinking it best to manage expectations.

For accuracy's sake, this was technically not Jimmy's first school dance. He had briefly attended a dance when he was in the eighth grade, a terrifying affair where the boys and girls lined up on either side of the school's basketball court. The glimmering lake of polished maple that separated them served as a Maginot Line no one dared cross except for precocious early adopters of dating who clung to each other at center court like lackadaisical zombies whenever the DJ played a slow song. The whole affair so frightened him that he fled out of the emergency exit after less than an hour and walked home to find refuge in another science fiction novel.

Mr. Watson's idea of monetizing the dance avoided this problem of preexisting couples dominating the dance floor. And because he insisted on a sliding fee scale—essentially an egalitarian "contribute what you can" approach—no one was excluded from participating in the fundraiser. It was a system that some parents on the organizing committee saw as a little too liberal, but those reservations were largely ignored.

As a result of these policies, nearly everyone ventured out onto the dance floor, and only the most exhausted dancers leaned against the chenille-covered walls of the old Harrison Price Hotel ballroom, swilling sweet pineapple-and-cranberry-flavored punch. For newly trained dancers like Jimmy, the nonstop dance floor activity that occurred between the featured fundraising dance segments was a godsend because it allowed him to practice his moves without anyone seeing him, especially the bullies who mainly stood around like vultures waiting for something or someone to criticize.

The band chosen for the dance, a group from Raleigh called The Five, was widely celebrated as the best high school band in the state. Most of the songs were reliable, danceable tunes, a mixture of pop classics, many suitable for beach dancing—something that Amanda had taught Jimmy to do. He hoped the band would choose one of these songs for his dance with Charlene since he'd have to hold her waist to spin her around, a thought that both terrified and thrilled him at the same time.

One of Jimmy's friends, Helen Hunter, agreed to dance with him as a warmup for his turn with Charlene. Helen was no-nonsense in these matters and showed Jimmy how to respectfully, but firmly, hold her close without getting "fresh," a term he sensed was out of date, but he knew what she meant.

"Put your left hand here at the small of my back," Helen said, guiding Jimmy's hand where it should go, pressing it firmly in place, "and use my right hand to maintain a respectable distance." Jimmy did as Helen directed, but then impressed her when he resolutely took the lead. Touching Helen's body so intimately felt strange because he had always thought of her more as a sister than as a girl. Helen sensed Jimmy's confusion and spoke up to reassure him. "Relax," she said. "It's OK. Just because we study together doesn't mean you can't touch me. We're just doing a different kind of studying." After that revelation, Jimmy relaxed and thought of Helen as a teacher and not a girl, a distinction he wasn't sure he understood at all.

One of the topics that had been brought up during the Panther fundraiser committee deliberations had been adding value to the event, or as Jason Miller, the owner of Miller's Variety Shop put it, "What will it take to motivate potential customers to buy a dance?"

Someone suggested a certificate of participation. Another committee member suggested giving participants (buyers and sellers) a T-shirt with the words *I Danced with* _____ printed on the front. After the featured dance segment, both participants would sign the blank space with special cloth pens. Fortunately, someone pointed out that buying T-shirts and pens would likely wipe out any profit they hoped to make. The idea was dropped immediately.

Then, the principal suggested a solution taken from ice-skating rinks and community pools where for a short period of time those who can actually skate or swim are allowed unfettered access to the facility. Applied to the dance event, Mr. Watson proposed clearing the dance floor at regular intervals. When the dance floor was clear, the emcee would announce the name of each fundraising participant and their partner as they walked toward a spotlight trained on the center of the dance floor. All dancers would get a round of applause at the end before the floor was opened up again to everyone. The committee immediately warmed to the idea, including Jason Miller, who said the idea was pure genius because it created happy customers who felt good about themselves and their choices.

While he waited for his name to be called, Jimmy carefully scrutinized Charlene's other partners. He noticed right away that his competitors were mediocre dancers at best, except for Charlene's two female dance partners who were quite accomplished and enthusiastic dancers. This gave him hope he could impress Charlene. He took care not to allow his growing confidence to cross a line into cockiness, which was something Amanda had counseled him against.

"I am never cocky when I'm performing," she told him toward the end of their lessons. "Confident, yes. Cocky, no. When cocky people fail, they fail badly. Confident people trust themselves and do their best so when they do fail, which is something everyone does, it generates empathy and people mostly forget about the failure. When cocky people fail, everyone is glad to see it happen." Amanda was something of a philosopher even then.

Jimmy's sister also gave him advice, but her counsel was about the need to "readjust things" in the restroom before meeting Charlene on the dance floor. Although he wasn't sure what readjusting entailed for girls—he assumed it wasn't something boys were supposed to know about—but whatever it was he naturally assumed boys probably needed a lot less of it. Still, he eventually took his sister's advice and went to the restroom to look himself over. He immediately understood what she meant when he saw himself in the mirror.

The person staring back at him looked as if he'd been wrestling cattle all day. His shirttail was out on both sides, and his hair, normally neatly combed, was sticking out in all directions. His tie was askew, and his jacket could not have been more wrinkled had he stuffed it in a sock drawer overnight. To his credit, he didn't panic, but calmly began smoothing out and hiding most of the wrinkles using the primping secrets his sister had shared with him.

"Girls have to be good at fixing flaws, so we look perfect all the time." Jane had said as she shared her techniques. "Boys don't think being put together is important, but it absolutely does matter, and it will make a difference to Charlene."

Jimmy expertly transformed the disheveled teenager who'd entered the restroom into a presentable, even handsome young man. He thought he'd nailed Amanda's definition of confidence. He made one final adjustment to his tie and was turning to leave when he heard someone walk into the elegant restroom with its gleaming white marble stalls, polished brass fixtures, and solid oak cabinetry. He didn't pay any special attention until he heard a familiar, but dreaded voice, and he immediately felt the air leave the room.

"Hey, Dumbo," the voice said, "you're looking sharp tonight—woo-eee—all dressed up and nowhere to go." The voice belonged to T.J. Hooper, one of the class bullies who had been harassing him since the third grade. Usually, T.J. traveled with two other tormentors, but for some reason he was alone and blocking the exit.

"Hi, T.J.," Jimmy said, with a friendly lilt in his voice, hoping T.J. would be satisfied with just humiliating him as he walked out the door. Unfortunately, T.J. didn't move.

"Where are you going?" T.J. said in a mock-friendly tone. "You don't want to stay here with me?" Jimmy took a step toward the door, and T.J. moved to block his way.

"Well, normally, that might be all right," Jimmy said, noticing his heart rate increasing and his skin getting warm, "but I have a dance coming up, so maybe some other time."

"Oh, you have a dance. That's nice. Who's your dance with?" T.J. said, his voice taking a harder, more mocking tone.

"Charlene Ravenport," Jimmy said, as he considered other escape routes.

"Oh, Charlene," T.J. said, with a predatory tone in his voice. "She's fine looking, even with those thick glasses. Is she your girlfriend?"

"No," Jimmy said tentatively, fear and anxiety gripping him as he thought about missing his dance with Charlene, "we're dancing for the fundraiser."

"Well, aren't you the ladies' man? Or maybe you're just one of the ladies," T.J. said, fully leaning into his bully persona. "Maybe I should take your dance. Would you mind that, Dumbo?"

Jimmy knew where this was going. T.J. would not let him leave the bathroom until he was tired of humiliating him, no matter how long it took. Or worse, he might force Jimmy into a fight that he'd lose before it started. In either case, he would miss his dance with Charlene. He was saddened beyond rage and realized he'd have to save himself and that he'd have to summon the same chutzpah that got him to the dance in the first place. Otherwise, all would be lost.

Thinking about this pivotal moment now, James can't imagine where the former Jimmy got the courage, but somehow his resolve was there waiting for him like an on-time train, so he climbed onboard.

"T.J.," Jimmy said, with more authority than he had ever said anything in his life. "I know what you are doing here, but I am not going to play this game. I am leaving, and if you want to pick a fight with me later, that's fine. You know where to find me. But right now, I will have my dance with Charlene, and there's no way in hell you're going to stop me. Do you understand?"

With that, he pushed past T.J. and confidently walked down the elegant hallway to the grand ballroom. T.J. stood frozen, framed by the restroom's doorway, and watched Jimmy walk away, stunned that someone had stood up to him—especially someone like Jimmy. Perhaps it was lingering confusion about what had happened in the restroom or perhaps he had a life-changing moment of introspection and self-awareness that rearranged his mean-spirited world, but for whatever reason, T.J. didn't look for Jimmy during or after the dance to settle the score.

"What happened to you?" Helen asked when Jimmy returned from the restroom. "Are you OK?"

"Yeah, sure," he said. "I just needed to readjust things like my sister suggested," putting emphasis on the word readjust.

"Well, you did a good job," she told him.

Just then, Mr. Watson took charge of the sound system and began reading the names of the next twenty couples who would occupy the dance floor. As the names of each couple were announced, the dancers stepped out of the crowd and walked toward a spotlight trained on the dance floor center as if they were movie stars on Oscars night, each getting generous encouragement from friends and fans. Then it was Jimmy's turn.

"Charlene Ravenport and Jimmy Johnson," Mr. Watson boomed in his best radio voice. A surprisingly loud cheer rose from the crowd. At first Jimmy wondered if he'd misheard his name, but Helen pushed him authoritatively out of the tightly packed crowd. Charlene emerged from the crowd on the opposite side of the dance floor, and as she did, she confidently waved to her fans as if she had won something. Jimmy waved to the crowd on his way to center stage, although not with the same confidence and enthusiasm as Charlene. She seemed to enjoy the attention.

The next time he was called on to wave to a large crowd was during his graduation when he crossed the stage three times. Once to get an award for his near-perfect grade point average and again to give his valedictorian speech. The third time was to accept Mr. Watson's congratulations for his full scholarship to Brown.

Despite practicing with Helen, Jimmy was unspeakably nervous when Charlene took his hand and raised it with hers in response to the crowd's cheers. He joined her in waving with his free hand, but beneath the smiles and surface enthusiasm he felt like running for the emergency exit again. He only started breathing when the spotlight moved away from them, its white-hot beam now trained on the next two dancers entering the stage.

"So nice to meet you," Charlene began. "Isn't this so much fun?!"

"I guess," he said. "I'm not used to waving at crowds."

"Just pretend it's your birthday party," she said. "At least that's what I do."

"I'll try that," he said, still unconvinced but glad he was now talking and not just standing there in awkward silence waiting for the music to start.

"You're a very good dancer," Jimmy said, as he desperately tried to think of something to say to break the uncomfortable silence.

"Thank you, and you're not so bad yourself," Charlene replied. "I noticed you dancing with Helen. Are you two dating?"

"Thanks," he said, suddenly nervous. "No, Helen and I are just good friends. We study math together, go to the movies once in a while, that sort of thing."

"Well, you two make a nice couple on the dance floor," she said, offering her comment as a simple statement of fact.

As it turned out, Jimmy and Helen did date the first summer he was home from Brown, but they parted ways by August when it became clear they were better at being friends. Besides, if they were honest with themselves, they knew they were engaged in nothing more than a sweet summer diversion that allowed for skinny-dipping late at night in the warm water of Lake Greenwood and sweaty afternoons of urgent, commitment-free sex.

Charlene and Jimmy were both relieved when Mr. Watson called the last dancers to the floor. The banter between them had been lively, but Jimmy was running out of topics beyond his favorite authors, movies, and plans for college.

Before handing the microphone to The Five's lead singer, Mr. Watson declared the dance an unqualified success. Everyone cheered. Then, as the principal left the stage, the first chords of the classic song, "Up on the Roof," filled the ballroom. A large, mirrored ball floating above the dance floor began to spin, reflecting red, green, and blue splotches of light onto the faces of the dancers and onlookers.

Jimmy smiled confidently. He offered Charlene his hand and immediately took charge with an authority that surprised them both. For the next three-and-a-half minutes, they fairly floated in and out of the white-hot spotlight—gliding, dipping, spinning, swaying—like two moths drawn to a bare lightbulb. Charlene's long auburn hair and its proximity to him was mesmerizing. It sparkled and gleamed when they danced through the spotlights as if she had braided it with tiny, electrified diamonds. He thought it was the most beautiful thing he'd ever seen in his short life.

Although he was completely seduced by the music and hoped it would never end, Jimmy began planning out his final spins and turns early so that when the last chord sounded their arms would be entwined with Charlene in front of him. It was a move he had once seen in a stage musical, and he nailed it perfectly.

Cheers erupted. Everyone clapped and whistled and called out "Woo-hoo." Charlene released Jimmy's hands and turned around to hug him. She kissed him enthusiastically on both cheeks.

"That was the best dance of the night," Charlene said, still looking a little flushed. "Where did you learn to dance like that? I'll dance with you anytime."

"Thanks," he said, before adding, "So if I asked you to dance the next song would you say yes?"

"Of course," she said, just as the drummer's rim shot announced the next tune, a solid pop standard that he and Amanda had used for their lessons. He knew just what to do.

Charlene and Jimmy danced together at least five times that evening, although Helen was still his principal partner. Helen advised him to play it cool and to not appear too eager, something she said girls hated. Jimmy spoke to Charlene when they were in close proximity but asked her to dance only when it seemed a natural, even unintentional result of their paths crossing. It was apparently the right strategic mix because it was during one of these brief interchanges that he asked Charlene out and she accepted. When he told Helen, she gave Jimmy a hug and congratulated him, but secretly she was a bit jealous and perhaps a bit hurt.

It would make a better story if Jimmy and Charlene's dance had led to a high school romance, but it didn't. After a few dates—movies, dinners, and a cotillion—they finally had their first kiss standing on the sidewalk outside Charlene's house. It was Jimmy's first real kiss, aside from an adolescent spin-the-bottle kiss he'd gotten during a Greenwood Baptist Church weekend retreat when he was in the ninth grade. Jimmy and Charlene continued to date fairly regularly, and even attended senior prom together, but kissing was as far as the romance progressed.

"Jimmy, you know I like you very much," Charlene said, one night after they'd kissed on the sidewalk in front of her house, "but you know we can only be friends. I just can't think of you in any other way. Do you know what I mean?"

"Sure, I think I do," Jimmy said, feeling a mixture of embarrassment and hurt, although he wasn't sure why. "So, you don't want to be my girlfriend, then."

"No," Charlene said, "I can't be that kind of girlfriend. We can go to the movies, go out dancing, go to parties together, but I am sorry, I just can't think of you as more than that."

"I understand," he said, feeling a lump grow in his throat.

"I knew you would," Charlene said. She kissed Jimmy on his cheek and said good night.

Of course, Jimmy was completely unaware of the difference between liking someone well enough to be their actual girlfriend and liking them well enough to just be friends. He only began to understand the difference his first year at Brown when he met Renée McCurdy, a free-spirited valedictorian from Vermont who demonstrated the concept to him one night in his dorm room after an orientation mixer with his roommate sleeping in the bed above them.

Still, he always thought of Charlene as one of the most important women in his life. The illusion of her perfection and his need to be with her had helped him push past two of his greatest fears: being in the spotlight and standing up to a bully who, as it turned out, was nothing more than a sad coward. And if the definition of success was customer satisfaction, then the dance, as far as Jimmy (James) Johnson was concerned, was nothing short of pure genius. Brilliant!

4

Marilee's Fishpond

STEWART PEABODY HAD BEEN PROMISING HIS WIFE, Marilee, for more than a year he would build a fishpond in their backyard. Then one day his excuses wore thin, and she threatened to call someone to "get it done." It was Marilee's one motivational ace in the hole that never failed to get her husband off the dime, as she liked to say.

To be fair, it wasn't laziness or lack of interest that made Stewart delay starting the fishpond project. Truthfully, given enough time Stewart *could* do almost any home project, and Marilee knew it. However, if twenty years of living with Stewart had taught her anything it was that a substantial gap existed between what her husband *could do* and what he actually *got done*.

For Stewart's part, he didn't think of himself as a procrastinator, but as someone who gave things what he called "due consideration." It was a fine point they had long ago agreed to disagree on. As for Marilee, she thought of herself as a doer: someone who put important tasks on a punch list in her head where they stayed, spinning around like a ham-and-cheese sandwich order clipped to a short order cook's ticket wheel, insistently spinning and endlessly worrying until the order was pulled down, cooked, and plated.

Marilee had gotten the idea of a fishpond when she and Stewart visited Biltmore Estate down in Asheville. She had marveled at the colorful koi (really just giant goldfish, she had thought) as they swam peacefully just under the surface of an Olympic-size pond. She loved watching the fish dart around and beneath blooming water lilies and the pond's tall, elegant grasses. Some of the fish were white and ghostlike, others mostly orange. A few sported red and orange splotches on a white background, a pattern that reminded her of the spotted ponies she and Stewart had seen when they took a trip to Assateague Island a few years earlier.

"Stewart," she said, not taking her eyes off the water, "don't you think a fishpond would be just the thing for our backyard?"

"Maybe," he said without much enthusiasm, knowing full well where this was going.

"Of course, it wouldn't have to be as grand as this," Marilee said, sweeping her hand expansively across the meticulously maintained pond before them.

"Just a small one—enough for a few fish and maybe some toads."

"I suspect I could," Stewart replied flatly, not wishing to encourage the idea.

"And I know just where it would go," Marilee continued. "Right under that big old oak tree where nothing grows except ivy and pachysandra."

"Well, it's something to consider," Stewart offered, hoping to buy some time.

It didn't.

4 – Marilee's Fishpond

On the way home, Marilee took out an old inspection receipt from the car's glove box and sketched a half dozen crude, but clear designs using a nearly dried-up but still working pen. She gave Stewart a chance to approve or reject each iteration, an opportunity he took to offer the advice that "simple is always better." Marilee soon figured out Stewart's strategy and stopped asking his opinion altogether.

Although it was late afternoon when they got home, Stewart agreed to help Marilee flesh out her best design ideas while they were clear in her mind. They spent an hour under the oak tree shaping and reshaping a length of garden hose until Marilee was satisfied that the shape and size matched her vision. She had Stewart mark off the pond's future perimeter using a can of white spray paint, then she ran inside to check the pond's orientation from the kitchen window.

On their way home from Asheville, Marilee had conjured up a fully realized vision of her fishpond. She imagined an oval shaped one, surrounded by a slate knee wall with a brick pathway snaking its way to the pond through a thick patch of pachysandra and hosta. She also thought a teak contemplation bench right next to her pond would be a nice touch. When she closed her eyes, she could almost hear the water rushing over a moss-covered outcrop of rocks flowing toward a crystal-clear pond full of blooming water lilies and of course contented, peaceful koi with coloring like Assateague ponies. She was ecstatic just thinking about it.

"It's perfect; thank you, sweetheart," Marilee called as she walked toward Stewart, who stood waiting for her patiently in a sea of pachysandra with the garden hose in one hand and the can of spray paint in the other. She gave Stewart a loving peck on the cheek and a hug.

"Glad to hear it, hon," Stewart said, reciprocating her affection, "So, if you're done here, I'll just put this hose and paint back in the garden shed, if you don't mind."

"That's fine," Marilee said, "but you should keep it handy just in case we need to refine the design." Stewart hung the garden hose on a hook just inside the door and put the paint next to it. He knew from experience he wasn't exactly done with the design phase of this project just yet.

The fishpond design phase was followed by a few months of sporadic discussion about the best time to start; and, as Stewart expected, a few adjustments to the pond's initial design were made. Then, suddenly, winter was upon them, which allowed Stewart the reasonable sounding caution that "winter was not the time to start a fishpond project." As a result, Marilee was forced to put the project on hold, a disappointment that allowed the fishpond-building ticket to keep spinning around in her head, annoying and insistent. But with the coming of the longer, more hopeful days of spring, Marilee's excitement about her fishpond project blossomed right along with her daffodils, crocuses, snowdrops, and bleeding hearts.

"Stewart," she said one morning while looking out the kitchen window with a contemplative, determined stare, "I was wondering, don't you think, especially with spring right around the corner, that now is the perfect time to start thinking about building our fishpond." It was a musing Stewart knew wasn't a question.

Stewart, who was sitting in his most comfortable chair reading the newspaper and drinking coffee, barely registered her comment and offered only a tepid "maybe-next-week" response. That's when Marilee rolled out her fail-safe nuclear option. "I understand you're busy," Marilee said nonchalantly, as if she were mentioning changing her hairstyle, "that's why I was thinking I'd call someone to come by this week to give us a bid. What do you think?"

4 – Marilee's Fishpond

Stewart sat up and folded the open newspaper in his lap. "Glad you mentioned it, hon," Stewart said. "Let me just go out and take some new measurements so we can finalize your plans."

"Are you sure?" Marilee said, a slight tinge of concern in her voice, a reaction that belied her utter joy at finally being able to pull down the annoying fishpond ticket and move on to something else.

"Oh, I'm sure," Stewart said, reconciling himself to the inescapable fact that his due consideration period was now officially over.

Truthfully, the fishpond building was a stretch project for Stewart. It was something he'd have to learn to do. *Still*, he thought, *how hard could it be?* He found a step-by-step guide in the Greenwood Public Library called *Fishpond Building Made Easy*. He used the book to create a construction plan that included a materials list and professional-looking elevation drawings that were, in his estimation, as good as those of any overpaid landscape architect.

His comprehensive materials list included an eighteen-foot, kidney-shaped, fiberglass pool liner (a design compromise that was substantially smaller than Marilee's original twenty-five-foot vision). He ordered two pallets each of brick and slate slabs for the path, patio, and knee wall; twenty bags of concrete; PVC pipes; water pumps; electrical wire; and other supplies. Once the materials were delivered, he staged them near the jobsite. Then he began to consider the biggest challenge of all: digging the hole.

One thing Stewart knew for sure was that chopping through well-established oak tree roots was impossible. He solved the problem by asking Sam Johnson to bring his human-size Bobcat backhoe over one Saturday morning in exchange for a bottle of Jack Daniel's. Sam was also a hunt club member who happened to own Greenwood's largest construction business.

Sam was happy to help—with or without the bottle of Jack—because Johnson Builders, Inc., had grown beyond the stage of Sam doing all the work. "Truth be told," he said to Stewart when he agreed to help, "I really miss playing with my toys, so I look at this more as recreation than work."

On the appointed day, Sam arrived with his human-size machine, which he'd tied down to a slightly bowed trailer he was towing with one of his company's heavy-duty trucks. After Sam backed the mini-backhoe off the trailer and onto the street, Stewart pointed to an open section in the fencing that surrounded his acre-size backyard.

"Take your toy through there," he directed his friend, "and try to avoid Marilee's garden. As I think you know, she's a bit protective of her children," he said with a good-natured chuckle.

※

The facts of what happened in Stewart's backyard after Sam started digging through a thicket of pachysandra and spidery oak tree roots is recorded in the June 15 edition of the *Greenwood Clarion* under the headline "Local Man Finds Gold Coins Digging Backyard Fishpond." It was a dramatic and compelling story, and it was pretty much all the news anyone talked about for quite some time.

Local Man Finds Gold Coins Digging Backyard Fishpond
Max Perkins, Features Editor

Greenwood Hardware and Supply Company manager Stewart Peabody said he was "in shock" over the discovery of the 350 double eagle gold coins he found in his backyard this past weekend while digging a fishpond for his wife.

"I guess we were about four feet down when we hit something that didn't look anything like roots," Peabody said, describing how he and Sam Johnson, owner of Johnson Builders, discovered the treasure. "At first, we thought it was an old drainage pipe, but when I scraped the dirt away, I found a rotting suitcase. I've never been more surprised in my life."

Peabody said Johnson used his backhoe to get the suitcase out into the light where it immediately disintegrated, spilling gold coins all over the ground like pirate's booty. "I don't mind telling you we were both speechless," Peabody said.

The two treasure hunters said they found nothing to identify who might have buried the treasure. "It's just baffling to me why someone would bury that much money and forget about it. I mean, it's not like misplacing your keys," Peabody reported.

Peabody said he planned to search Greenwood land and deed records in an effort to find the treasure's original owner. If that search was fruitless, Peabody said he might sell the coins and use the money to hire a landscaping company to finish his fishpond.

"Frankly, I was not that excited about this project in the first place, with or without finding buried treasure," Peabody confessed. "Doing brick and slate work is a stretch for me if I am honest."

By all accounts, Peabody should have an exceptionally generous budget for his fishpond. According to local coin collector Sy Jones, owner of The Coin Collector Shop on Main Street, a single pre-1933 double eagle coin is worth between $1,800 and $2,800, or in street value terms between $630,000 and $980,000 for all the coins. Now, that's some backyard fishpond budget, for sure!

The *Clarion* article made Stewart and Sam local celebrities. A photograph accompanying the article showed Stewart and Sam holding up cupped handfuls of shiny double eagle coins, both men smiling ear to ear. In the days that followed, Stewart spent a good portion of his day at the hardware store retelling the story of how he'd found the coins, often deflecting ludicrous suggestions about the best way to spend his newfound wealth.

For a time, he kept a single coin in his pocket encased in a protective plastic holder that Sy had given him so he could offer his best customers and friends a chance to see one of the coins. Most examined it like it was a holy relic, turning it over gingerly in the palms of their hands as if to avoid damaging it. Occasionally, he used the coin to rid himself of people who refused to stop talking. "Hey, I got to get back to work," he'd say, "but how would you like to see one of those double eagles before you go?" It was an effective and not overly rude send-off, Stewart thought.

A week after the *Clarion* article appeared, a reporter for the *News & Observer* in Raleigh drove down to interview Stewart and Sam. The article, published in the Sunday edition, prompted a crew from the capital's most-watched television station to film an interview with the treasure hunters. A second wave of celebrity ensued.

Unsurprisingly, landscaping companies started calling day and night—a problem Stewart solved by putting Marilee in charge of taking the calls. "Just remember," he told her. "We don't live at the Biltmore Estate, so any extras like speakers embedded in knee walls or special rocks imported from Italy we don't need, but short of that, knock yourself out."

When Stewart finally got down to City Hall to look at land and deed records, he discovered that all the surrounding land had once belonged to the Price family, early wealthy residents of Greenwood.

4 – Marilee's Fishpond

His house, a single-story Arts and Crafts style, built by Hiram Jenkins and his wife Rachel in 1949, sat on Price land that had been subdivided into single-family lots in the early 1930s. Hiram and Rachel raised three children, Gladys, Glen, and Samuel, in the house and lived there until moving to a retirement home.

After that, the house had been rented out until Stewart and Marilee bought and renovated it. All three Jenkins children still lived in town, and each said they were as surprised as everyone else about the treasure. "Believe me," Gladys, the oldest child joked when Stewart called her, "if my father had given me a treasure map on his deathbed, I'd have dug it up while WE owned the house!"

※

Harrison James Price, the patriarch of the Price family, moved to Greenwood in 1880 from Albany, New York. Even then, he was considered a carpetbagger when he bought a lavishly constructed antebellum home and three hundred acres of land that abutted the Green family's property. In time, Price became a prominent businessman, second only to the direct descendants of Lester Hamilton Green, who had built an imposing mansion on the highest hill in the 1850s and was considered the founder of Greenwood. At one time, in addition to his farm operation, Price owned one of Greenwood's two general stores and the town's only hotel, the Harrison Price Hotel.

The current Price descendant was Sebastian Price, a youngish widower who lived on the last twenty acres of his great-grandfather's original estate. Much of it was transformed into manicured gardens with a well-defined riding path that allowed Sebastian to wear traditional livery and gallop across the lush landscape like English nobility.

It was a privileged lifestyle most people in Greenwood didn't understand, given that Sebastian never specifically said what he did for a living, only that he dabbled a bit in the stock market. It was a curious explanation because even those who knew nothing about investing understood it took more than *dabbling* to afford the expensive cars he drove, the lavish vacations he took, and the Gatsby-like parties he sometimes threw at his estate.

Sebastian was sitting in one of his freshly painted vintage Brumby Rockers that lined his home's grand veranda when he read the *Clarion* article about Stewart's treasure. He nearly dropped the weighty Waterford glass he was holding a bit too carelessly in his right hand as he shot straight out of his seat like something had stung him. "Oh, my God," he yelped, spinning around, spilling ice and the watery remains of his artisanal bourbon, "those are Grandpa Benjamin's gold coins. No doubt about it!"

The reason Sebastian was convinced the coins belonged to his great-grandfather was because he had lived with the legend of Benjamin Price's lost treasure his entire life. As the story went, in the summer of 1929 Benjamin Price, Sebastian's great-grandfather, was a high-flying investor who, like the rest of the Wall Street elite at the time, thought the profits party would never end. Benjamin, however, had serious doubts.

In fact, he was so worried about losing all his money he told his wife Amelia, Sebastian's great-grandmother, out of the blue one day that he had buried "as many twenty-dollar gold pieces as he could find" in a nearby field "just in case it all went to hell." He told his wife about his stock market fears and advised her to use the money to save herself and the family if something should ever happen to him or his money. Benjamin didn't explain where he'd chosen to bury the gold coins, only that he'd leave a map to the treasure in the family safe. Sebastian thought of his great-grandfather as a slightly off, modern-day survivalist, someone wealthy enough to spend millions renovating an abandoned nuclear

4 – Marilee's Fishpond

missile silo to escape the coming wholesale collapse of society.

Unfortunately, Benjamin died of a heart attack before completing his treasure map, or so it seemed, because no map was ever found in or outside his safe. However, a brass surveyor's instrument was found on top of a pile of important financial documents in the safe, a quirky family heirloom that Sebastian now used as a paperweight on his desk.

Fortunately, at least for future Price family descendants, Benjamin had followed his instincts and shorted most of his market positions before Black Tuesday came in October of 1929. Formerly high-flying, now broke, investors jumped out of office buildings, banks closed their doors, many permanently, and millions of Americans lost their jobs. But the Price family and its heirs got even richer. As for the gold coins buried on the Price estate, c'est la vie, as the saying goes.

Still, the lost treasure story had given two generations of Price children something to do as they traipsed around the family property with shovels and pickaxes swung over their shoulders like they were characters in one of Mark Twain's stories, forever digging holes indiscriminately, all the while utterly convinced that every random mound of dirt or divot in the earth was surely the right spot.

Sebastian was still a treasure hunter in many ways, only now he dug with his Ivy League financial acumen to unearth undervalued stocks that he bought and sold at the most opportune times. He couldn't say why he had danced a jig the day he read about Stewart Peabody's find. It wasn't because he needed the money. If anything, it was about vindication: first, that his childhood fantasies were real, and second, that someone had finally, after all this time, dug in the right spot.

※

Sebastian would have called Stewart Peabody sooner had he been home to read of Stewart's discovery. As it was, he had been in New York attending a board meeting, and so two weeks passed until he was able to sift through a large wicker basket of mail that his housekeeper always collected in his absence. Normally, he'd have found the *Clarion* in a basket reserved for catalogs, newspapers, and junk mail, most of it he might have ignored given its volume, so it was a simple stroke of luck that Sebastian had even seen the article.

Sebastian called the *Clarion* publisher, Larry Fine, a personal friend who had attended at least one of his famous parties, to tell him the news.

"Larry, this is Sebastian Price," he said when his friend answered. "You won't believe what I'm about to tell you. You know those gold coins Stewart Peabody found in his backyard? First, I know who buried them—my great-grandfather, Benjamin James Price—and I know when he did it, sometime before October of 1929."

Sebastian gave the newspaper publisher a synopsis of his family's buried treasure lore and explained how he and his cousins spent their summers searching for the lost gold coins. Larry Fine arranged an interview the next day with the *Clarion*'s feature editor who asked Sebastian to gather any relevant documents and photos ahead of their interview.

After hanging up, Larry Fine leaned back in his chair and put his feet on top of the galley proof he was reading. He shook his head and blew out a lungful of air, pursing his lips just enough to make a faint whistle that sounded like a strong wind racing down a narrow alley. "Woo-eee, now that's some story," he said to himself. Then he called Stewart Peabody at the hardware store.

"Stewart," he said, "this is Larry Fine at the *Clarion*. I just talked with Sebastian Price, and you're not going to believe what he just told me about those gold coins you found!"

4 – Marilee's Fishpond

The following week the *Clarion* published a front-page article explaining how Stewart's find had solved a century-old mystery for the Price family. Now, both Sebastian and Stewart were the talk of the town, and not the proposed water and sewer tax hike that had until then fully occupied the collective anger and outrage of the town's taxpaying citizenry.

Sebastian stopped by the hardware store a few days later, and he and Stewart had a friendly conversation. They avoided direct discussion about ownership of the coins, but they did agree to meet the following week at Sebastian's estate to discuss what he called "the disposition of the coins."

It was all reasonable and civilized conversation, and everyone just assumed Stewart and Sabastian would "work it out." What *working it out* meant ranged from Stewart just turning over the coins for a small finder's fee, to expecting nothing at all (aka, the Christian solution), to a strict application of the less charitable "finders keepers, losers weepers" rule.

It's important to note that the consensus skewed mightily toward the latter outcome, especially if Sebastian Price were the loser. Then, as Larry Fine says, even years later when recounting the story, all hell broke loose when the *Clarion* published a long letter to the editor submitted by Melvin P. Bacon Esq., a local real estate and contract law attorney. Melvin pointed out in elegantly constructed legalese that "regardless of where the gold coins were found or any providential evidence that may or may not be offered by a claimant, including family legends and folklore, the ultimate ownership rights of any valuable or historic treasure must be determined by law enforcement officials and the courts, not the finder of the treasure or any other claimant to it."

Melvin's letter had two immediate effects. First, it galvanized the finders-keepers faction and turned what once seemed a simple and neighborly transaction into just another example of overreach by meddling government bureaucrats and sleazy, lying lawyers. As such, the consensus opinion of a good portion of townsfolk began to tilt toward what local curmudgeon, Junior Blandly, said one afternoon while he sipped his coffee at Dixie's Diner.

"I will tell you this," he said succinctly and with a certainty that belied his lack of direct experience. "Once these institutions and professions get involved, you can bet your ass there won't be enough left of those gold coins to buy a cup of coffee between them—and that's an absolute fact."

The other, closer-to-home impact of Melvin's letter in the *Clarion* was that Marilee stopped getting calls from landscaping firms, although a few did send scaled-down versions of their original bids without knee wall speaker systems, underwater lights, complicated waterfall features, and other bells and whistles that Stewart had warned Marilee against considering in the first place.

To be fair, it had never been Melvin Bacon's intention to throw a wrench into the feel-good narrative that had been circulating among the Greenwood populace ever since the coins' discovery. But as he saw it, someone had to point out the simple truth that no one can really own anything until the legal guidelines that govern society allow such ownership. There must always be a paper trail of who owns what. Even the Romans, the Egyptians, and the Sumerians before them, understood this fundamental truth given the vast numbers of stone, papyrus, and clay tablet receipts detailing purchases, transfers of ownership, bills of sale, and promissory notes each civilization left behind for archaeologists to find. What surprised Melvin more than anything was that no one had bothered to point this basic fact of life out before he did.

His letter, which occupied more than a quarter of the *Clarion*'s Letters to the Editor page, laid out precisely why civilizations needed well-defined economic rules of engagement. He cited case law going back a hundred years to back up his points and offered his personal experience in these matters, noting with a bit of non-lawyerly flair that "if twenty years of legal work has taught me anything, it is that money, even small amounts of it, always ruins the pie—every single time. And in this case, with a potentially huge pie to divide, the risk of making an awful mess of it is exceptionally high."

After reading Melvin's letter, Stewart was not surprised to see Greenwood's chief of police, Jim Jenson, and two other officers walk into his hardware store a few days later. Jim told Stewart that the gold coins must be turned over until his office could "investigate the circumstances of the coins' discovery and every attempt was made to determine the rightful owner." Stewart did not protest. He pulled his show-and-tell double eagle out of his pocket and handed it over.

Then they all walked down to the Greenwood Community Bank where Stewart had stored the rest of the coins a month earlier in his bank deposit box. Sy had given Stewart special sleeves to protect the coins and a professional archival storage box to keep them in. Jim accompanied Stewart into the bank vault where he took possession of the coins but not without regret.

"Sorry, Stewart," Jim said, careful not to sound apologetic. "It's the procedure we have to follow in cases such as these. I'm sure you understand."

"Yes, Jim," Stewart said flatly and without emotion. "You're just doing your job."

And that was true up to a point, but a less agreeable part of Stewart wanted to ask Jim why he hadn't said anything about such legal requirements when he had come by the hardware store the previous weekend to buy a box of twelve-gauge shotgun shells or later when he'd asked excitedly to see the famous double eagle coin. It was not a question Stewart could answer, other than to say that perhaps the sheriff was wearing a different hat that day.

Conflagrations never end well, especially ones fueled by money, jealousy, misinformation, misunderstanding, and a general dissatisfaction about the order of things.

The first incendiary spark was the elegantly crafted letter by Melvin Bacon reminding everyone that nothing, not even the joyous discovery of gold coins and the solving of a hundred-year-old mystery, was as simple as it first appeared. The next piece of kindling thrown on the fire was the letter Sebastian's lawyer sent to Stewart officially declaring that Sebastian's great-grandfather, Benjamin James Price, had a rightful claim to the coins and that the Price estate intended to ask the courts to award the coins to his direct heir, Sebastian Price.

In fairness to Sebastian, he had not wanted any of this to happen. After visiting the hardware store, he had genuinely believed that Stewart would do the right thing once he was presented with the evidence: references in old letters, testimonies from family members, and perhaps other documents he expected to uncover.

In Sebastian's mind at least, doing the right thing meant giving Stewart a reasonable, but substantial finder's fee, certainly enough to hire the best landscaping company to finish his fishpond project. He was also willing to offer the use of his attorney if any tax liability questions came up. However, now that the coins were in "the system,"

4 – Marilee's Fishpond

Sebastian had no choice but to play the game by less flexible and certainly less agreeable rules.

Stewart went home after handing the coins over to Jim Jenson and told Marilee he was starting to wish he'd never found the treasure in the first place. Between the newspaper interviews he'd done, the dozens of times he'd told the treasure-finding story, and the hours he'd spent reviewing stacks of contracts sent by companies clamoring to build his fishpond, Stewart complained that he couldn't remember the last time he'd thought about anything else.

"This was a lot more fun when Sam and I first dug up those damn coins," he said to Marilee, "when the only value they had to us was the excitement of finding them. Now, I don't know. There's not much joy in this anymore, and now it looks like I am still the one building your fishpond—not that I mind, you understand."

Marilee had no solution or suggestion to ameliorate the current state of affairs except to say that a considerable number of her friends had suggested to her that in hindsight she and Stewart probably should have put the whole lot in a shoebox under their bed and labeled it "rainy day fund" and never told a soul.

"But now that the cat is out of the bag," she continued, in a tone that suggested she'd already made up her mind about what she was about to say, "I guess the best *we* can do is hire our own lawyer to make sure we are not paying Sebastian Price for the trouble *we* caused *him* by digging up his great-grandfather's treasure." She emphasized the words *we* and *him* to make sure her point was clear.

Marilee's suggestion echoed a widely held point of view that government in general—and lawyers in particular—were themselves the problem, not the solution, and should only be called on as a last resort.

"I do appreciate what that lawyer wrote about everyone following a mutually agreed set of rules and facts," Marilee said, "but it seems to me that you and Sebastian could have worked this out between yourselves, and at the very least he'd have paid for my fishpond as a reward. As it is, all I see out my kitchen window is a muddy hole slowly filling up with leaves."

"I understand how you feel," Stewart said, "but I still think we've got to trust the system. Who knows, it might surprise us," he concluded hopefully.

"Well, I'm not holding my breath," she replied, dismissing the discussion for now.

※

Sebastian's aunt, Eunice Fitzgerald Price Parker, was the Price family packrat. She was someone who collected and cataloged every significant fact about the Price family dating back to the early eighteenth century: newspaper articles, marriage licenses, legal documents, and correspondence, to name just a few categories. She also maintained an up-to-date family tree—a proud family history that was reflected in a framed illustration of a leafless tree with hundreds of calligraphed names sprouting off its sturdy main and secondary branches, each name with a birth, marriage, and death date recorded for every generation. It was an impressive network of familial ties that looked like chicken scratch from a distance.

Eunice knew the family lore about her great uncle's buried treasure, but she had dismissed it like everyone else as nothing more than a colorful story she dredged up occasionally to tell at cocktail parties. Then, Sebastian sent her a copy of the *Clarion* article with Stewart's and Sam's picture on the front page. Suddenly her packrat ways took on a new meaning as she was the only family member who could answer two essential questions that generations of Price family members had asked. First, what happened to Benjamin Price's treasure map—if there ever was one? And second, what possessed a normally stable and thoughtful financial professional to bury a treasure in the middle of a field somewhere rather than invest it?

As Eunice engaged in her detective work, clear battle lines formed in Greenwood. Stewart was largely on the side of those who gave both government institutions and lawyers the benefit of the doubt, but he was in the smaller group. For those on the other side, Stewart was the victim of a corrupt, cumbersome system and Sebastian was the greedy, rich oppressor unwilling to share his wealth with anyone else.

The *Greenwood Clarion* published a series of letters that made the case for one side or the other. Some of the arguments were reasonably stated, while others were a jumble of angry rants about individual rights and how the controversy was an example of the country going to "h— in a handbasket" (these were good Christian ranters, after all).

Larry Fine wrote an editorial supporting Melvin Bacon's point of view, stating that the disposition of the treasure was a matter for the legal system. Although a great number of readers wrote to say they disagreed with him, only a few canceled their subscriptions. Out in the community, citizens were heard discussing their points of view—mostly respectfully but not always—on the streets, in the town's shops and restaurants, and even before and after church services at the Greenwood Baptist Church where Stewart and Marilee were members.

During this vigorous community debate, Stewart and Sebastian stayed on the sidelines, but secretly Sebastian's thoughts began to drift toward Stewart's frustrated point of view that *finding* treasure was not as rewarding or interesting as *searching* for it. Plus, Sebastian was genuinely hurt by the controversy. He broached with his lawyer the idea of publicly telling his side of the story in an op-ed, a notion his lawyer discouraged with lawyerly candor and insight.

"I would advise against that, Sebastian," his lawyer told him. "Rich people are not a class of people that non-rich people have much sympathy for, if you know what I mean."

"From their point of view, any complaints from you about unfair treatment would sound as laughable to them as someone who always eats their perfectly cooked steak off fine bone china in an opulent, gilded dining room and then one day complains about the meat being slightly overcooked. I don't think that dog will run."

While Stewart waited for the court hearing, he cleaned out the leaves and debris that had fallen into Marilee's unfinished fishpond excavation. He had to work around the yellow crime scene tape that Jim Jenson had used to cordon off the area after he'd confiscated the gold coins. It was clearly an unnecessary use of tape, although Jenson seemed thrilled to have a crime scene of any kind to cordon off.

Then, Stewart began working again on Marilee's fishpond. First, because it distracted him from the controversy of the gold coins, and second, because he'd determined that if Sebastian did give him a reward, it wouldn't be enough to hire a proper landscaper and crew, even after he subtracted the speaker systems and dancing fountains that some of the bids contained. And besides, once he started working on her pond again, Marilee's mood improved and her enthusiastic nature returned, which was certainly something worth celebrating.

4 – Marilee's Fishpond

Eunice Price knew exactly where to begin investigating the mystery of her great uncle's buried treasure. One of the fortunate things about having a six-bedroom, turn-of-the-century mansion just outside Greenwich, Connecticut, was storage space; and Eunice had that in spades.

Family members had learned over the years to send Eunice every box of family correspondence and memorabilia they came across rather than toss it. She meticulously sorted through all the boxes that came her way, labeling each for later reference and saving obviously important documents for future Price generations.

She kept a cross-referenced ledger listing all her holdings, precisely noting where every entry was stored, a necessary habit given that two of her bedrooms were already chockablock with file cabinets, storage bins, and unsorted cardboard boxes. Such fastidiousness was why uncovering the secrets of Benjamin Price's life required only a single morning of ledger searching. She easily found five sturdy boxes labeled Benjamin Price—Greenwood, N.C. that were stored in the western corner of the blue room.

Eunice discovered that Benjamin Price and her grandfather, Oscar Peterson Price, regularly corresponded with each other. What she read revealed two men who were keen on keeping each other abreast of family life, noting news of travels, births, purchases (Oscar had bought a 1928 Packard Runabout in July of that year), and the untimely deaths of friends and colleagues.

Then, in early 1929, Benjamin began writing about the overvalued stock market, even worrying in one letter that if nothing changed "everyone was going to lose their shirts." Eunice's grandfather didn't share his brother's worry at first, but eventually he took on Benjamin's concerns and reported in a letter to Benjamin that he too planned to short all his market positions. It was a decision that ultimately saved Oscar's fortune and allowed his granddaughter to live in a fine mansion with lots of unused bedrooms.

One letter was particularly intriguing. Dated June 15, 1929, the letter (from Benjamin to Oscar) was a long soliloquy on the current state of the stock market, rich in technical detail and ending with a shockingly prescient prediction: "The market will fail by the end of the year. I am convinced of it." Then came a clue that almost made Eunice fall out of her chair when she read it.

"I don't think we will convince many of our colleagues to take the same dramatic action we have," Benjamin wrote. "It might be a dangerous and foolish strategy to bet ours and our family's lives on, all for something I cannot prove to be true except by relying on my experience and intuition. Nevertheless, I remain convinced and feel it prudent to take a small precaution against our bet, the details of which I will provide you in another letter. For now, take care to safeguard this important set of letters and numbers."

"My God in heaven," Eunice said, "if that isn't proof, then I don't know what is."

Eunice called Sebastian immediately and read the passage to him. When she was done, they both jumped around like they were auditioning for the part of Humphrey Bogart in the movie *The Treasure of the Sierra Madre.*

"That's all I've found for now," Eunice told Sebastian after she stopped dancing and had her breath, "but I still have more boxes to go through."

"I'd say that's a good day's work, Eunice," Sebastian said, "but you know, I have to wonder why no one else knew about this letter."

4 – Marilee's Fishpond

"I'm sure someone else must have read it before now," Eunice replied. "My grandfather for one, obviously, but remember, Benjamin died that fall, a few months after sending it, so I suspect looking through old letters wasn't a top priority for a family who had gotten richer, not poorer, after the worst financial crisis in US history."

The story of how Sebastian figured out the meaning of his great-grandfather's secret code turned on two unique factors about him: his Ivy League education and his investor skills, which gave him the tenacity of a treasure hunter. But more than anything, solving the mystery of Benjamin's cryptic code required a bit of luck, something he got from a very unexpected place, so close to him that if it had been a snake, it would have bit him.

Prior to having his epiphany, Sebastian worked through the numbers and symbols Eunice sent him like an obsessed conspiracy theorist. He covered a wall of his office with dozens of colored sticky notes looking for connections between his great-grandfather's clues and the treasure. His conclusion after a day of work was that "it didn't tell me a goddamn thing."

Then, luck played its hand when he picked up the old surveyor's compass that had been in his grandfather's safe. He was about to place another stack of bills under the heavy heirloom when he hesitated. Perhaps it was the weight of the vintage brass instrument, but as he set it back down on top of the documents, the answer occurred to him like a message from God.

"You idiot," he said, sitting down hard in his office chair. Those numbers are coordinates on a map. Any surveyor or landowner would know that. Benjamin Price, you were a true genius, except, of course, for falling over dead before finishing your map," he added with a slight chuckle.

※

Stewart was blissfully unaware of Eunice's and Sebastian's detective work. He worked weekends and evenings after closing the hardware store to finish Marilee's fishpond and was generally pleased with himself, both for his work and for not having paid someone else to do it. Besides, he didn't hate doing the project nearly as much as he had thought he would.

In town, the controversy over who owned the gold coins had subsided somewhat, and all the disgust and anger about it was transferred to government bureaucrats championing unwarranted tax increases and the installation of a new traffic light on Main Street. Larry Fine even stopped getting letters about Stewart's treasure, but he fully expected that once the result of the court hearing was published, he'd get an earful.

As the weeks passed and the hearing date drew near, Marilee watched Stewart install the first three runs of gray flagstones from her kitchen window. Stewart ended up wiring the pond for underwater lights and installed two additional outdoor outlets after Marilee pointed out that adding lights was a relatively small expense considering he'd already dug the water supply trench and added a new circuit to the house electrical panel for the pond's water pumps. Stewart couldn't argue with that logic.

Sebastian continued building his case with Eunice's help, and a land survey company confirmed the accuracy of his great-grandfather's treasure coordinates. Essentially, it was a reverse-engineering puzzle that assumed Stewart's fishpond was a known point on a map. His lawyers also gathered historical land and deed documents and photographs taken before Stewart's house and dozens of other houses in the neighborhood were built, all potential backup for Sebastian's claim of ownership.

Such extra documentation was hardly needed once the land survey company handed Benjamin its final report. The facts of the case were clear: Benjamin Price had indeed gathered a huge cache of US eagle gold coins in 1929 and buried them in what would one day be Stewart Peabody's backyard.

The day of the hearing Stewart dressed appropriately in one of his better Sunday suits and a red tie to show his respect for the institution. Marilee was dressed in customary fashion—to the nines. His lawyer had advised him to simply tell the truth about the circumstances of finding the gold coins. He would do the rest. Sam Johnson would testify if needed. Stewart didn't much think he needed a lawyer, but Marilee's argument about not being liable in any way for simply digging up the coins did worry him on some level.

Sebastian arrived as always, dressed like someone who never looked at price tags. His entourage included several lawyers, Eunice Price, the leader of the survey team, and a few expert witnesses to verify salient facts about his ownership case. Sebastian was uncomfortable using such overwhelming legal force to prove his case, but his lawyer said that without a decisive judgment concerning legal ownership of the coins, no one would own them. "Get the coins awarded to you," his lawyer had said, "and after that you can do what you want with them. Give them to meals-on-wheels if you like, but somebody's gotta own the treasure officially and you're the best candidate for that job."

These fine points of the law were not exactly salient factors to the more than 150 people who crowded into the small civil courtroom at Greenwood City Hall or spilled out into the hallway. A few were just curious onlookers who had no opinion about the case. Still, the vast majority were rooting for Stewart to win and for Sebastian to lose. Some of the local citizenry took time to make signs in support of Stewart's cause, even though Stewart didn't think of himself as having any cause to rally around.

Stewart's and Sebastian's lawyers each made opening statements that set out their positions, then both sides made their cases. Stewart's portion of the hearing lasted no more than fifteen minutes and consisted of him stating the circumstances of how he and Sam Johnson had found the coins.

Sebastian's portion of the hearing lasted nearly an hour and included more than a dozen exhibits: letters, historical photographs, sworn testimony from Price family members about the gold coin legend, and, crucially, testimony from Sebastian's surveyor who explained in detail how he had pinpointed the gold coins' location using the coordinates found in Benjamin Price's letter.

It was pretty much a slam-dunk presentation, and no one was surprised at all with the judge's decision. In fact, the presentation was so convincing that even those who had been angry with the process before the hearing had to admit that Sebastian had a legitimate claim to the treasure, though for some it was just another example of the old adage "Them that's got, get."

Stewart and Sebastian shook hands after the hearing, and Stewart congratulated him on his win, although it still irked him that such a dog-and-pony show had even been necessary. After the hearing he went back to the hardware store to finish his day and that evening put another round of stones on his fishpond knee wall. It was calming work that he was grateful to have.

A few weeks after the hearing, Stewart got a letter from Sebastian along with a check for $150,000. He was so shocked that he almost threw the letter away thinking it was junk mail informing the lucky "any resident" that "you may have just won $1 million!"

Once he had regained his wits, he ran out to the backyard where Marilee was sitting on the slate knee wall talking to her newly released koi family, Fred, Francis, and Frank (there was no reason for the names, other than she thought it was funny).

"Marilee, you won't believe what I just got in the mail from Sebastian," he said.

"What," Marilee said, "a note thanking us for the million dollars?"

"Hardly," he said, "a check for $150,000."

Marilee's jaw dropped.

"I'm not kidding," he said, handing her the check.

She turned the check over and held it up to the light. "Seems legit enough. Why would he do that?" Marilee asked, letting a little excitement enter her voice.

"You want me to read the letter to you?" Stewart asked.

"Sure," Marilee said, getting up from the knee wall to sit on the teak contemplation bench Stewart had made for her.

Dear Stewart and Marilee,

I am sorry to not have gotten this to you sooner, but I had to leave town immediately after the hearing, and it took some time for me to officially take legal possession of the coins. I hope you will find the enclosed check useful and that it makes up for any hard feelings or trouble caused by your discovery of my great-grandfather's gold coins.

For some reason, everyone in town seems to think I wanted the coins for their monetary value, but the truth is I was more interested in solving the mystery of my great-grandfather's treasure than anything else. For me, solving the riddle was the fun part; the part I didn't enjoy was the discord it caused around town.

One reason I'm writing is to let you know that I've created a charitable foundation, Greenwood Treasure Chest, that I will fund using the sale of the coins you found. The purpose of the foundation will be to award college scholarships to promising high school students interested in pursuing a business career. My great-grandfather was a very savvy finance guy and he would be happy to know the proceeds of his investment will be used for this worthy purpose.

You will read about the foundation and the finder's fee check in an article Larry Fine is writing for the *Greenwood Clarion*. I tell you this because Larry will likely call you to get your comments for the article.

In the meantime, thank you and Marilee for helping the Price family solve this century-old mystery.

Best regards,
Sebastian Price

"Well, what do you know about that?" Stewart said. "That's very generous of Sebastian. Don't you think?"

"Sure," Marilee said, turning the check over in her hand. "I guess all's well that ends well, as they say."

"It's a shame, though," Marilee said, a slight smile forming on her face. "Had we gotten this money before you finished, we could be listening to our garden speaker system, and we'd still have money left over."

"You just never give it up, do you?" he said, a little twinkle in his eyes.

"No, I guess not," she said. "It's not really in my nature. But you have to admit, it's nice to have this fishpond, even if you had to build it."

"Yes, it is," Stewart said, agreeing. Then he added, "And if you really want music, I can bring home some of those outdoor speakers we sell in the store that look like ordinary rocks."

"That's sweet of you to offer, hon," Marilee said, "but we can have them installed in the gazebo I've been thinking we need over there." She pointed to an area behind Stewart and handed him a sheet of paper with several nicely executed designs on the front and back.

"It's a good idea, Marilee," Stewart said, as calmly as possible. "Perhaps that might be a project for next year. For now, let's just enjoy our fishpond."

Marilee smiled and stood up to hug her agreeable husband. Stewart lovingly reciprocated her affection. Then they sat down together to watch their giant goldfish swim peacefully through the crystal-clear pond water and glide effortlessly beneath and around the pond's newly installed grasses and water lilies.

He had to admit that Marilee was right, a fishpond in their backyard was "just the thing." However, when he thought about Marilee's gazebo idea he immediately and resolutely began twisting the due consideration timer in his head until he thought the spring would break. Then, like it was some calming talisman, he ran his index finger around the edges of Sebastian's check and after a few rounds, managed to crack a smile.

5

Sara Jean's Bees

IN RETROSPECT, MERLE FLACK SHOULD NEVER HAVE agreed to carry a colony of his sister Sara Jean's honeybees in his car between Greenwood and her new home ten miles north of town.

It was an especially bad idea given Merle's lifelong fear of bees, an understandable aversion undoubtedly related to his stepping on a yellow jacket nest when he was ten years old. Even now, Merle clearly remembers the searing pain of the bee stings and the sound of his mother's sobs as she held his head in her lap in the backseat of the family sedan while his father sped to Greenwood Hospital in full panic mode, blaring his horn as he ran through every red light along the way.

It was fortunate that Merle wasn't allergic to bee stings, otherwise he surely would have died, at least according to the attending physician. As it was, he was given a generous dose of Benadryl and sent home a few hours later "as good as new." A true enough assessment disregarding, of course, the debilitating trauma that still drove his irrational fear of bees.

How Merle got such an ill-suited job in the first place is due in large part to Merle's kind and compassionate heart, something that made it hard for him to say no when someone asked for his help. Not that there's anything wrong with helping people out in need. It's just that Merle tended to volunteer before he took time to fully consider the potential consequences of his acquiescence.

In this case, his sister was in a bind. A confluence of circumstances had left everyone in their family, except Merle, unavailable to help move the last of Sara Jean's "fragile things" to her new house, mainly heirloom crystal and china and, of course, her beloved honeybees.

She had called Merle a week earlier in a tizzy of frustration complaining that everyone was too busy to help, so she had fairly pleaded with her brother to help her out. Although Merle planned to take the day off from work to cast for bass on Lake Greenwood, he agreed to help, thinking he might still have time to cast a few lines in the late afternoon.

A few years ago, Merle volunteered to drive a rental truck full of his parent's belongings to a senior living facility near Jacksonville, Florida. But here again, Merle's selfless, well-intentioned act of kindness and familial love had not gone to plan. First, the truck broke down outside of Savannah and the wait for repairs had cost him a day. Then there was a two-day move-in delay at the retirement facility due to some scheduling snafu, which precipitated a cascade of business and personal consequences for Merle. One of which was a significant shortening of a long-planned anniversary trip to a luxury mountain resort with his wife LeeAnn.

Although Merle admitted to being a bit annoyed about the turn of events, he generally took such setbacks in stride, something LeeAnn was less able to do.

Greenwood

"It seems to me, Merle," his wife told him when he called to deliver the disappointing news, "that you're always the one left holding the proverbial bag. Maybe next time you'll see fit to let someone else have a turn."

To be fair, Merle's current bag-holding situation was more a consequence of proximity than choice and of course his penchant for doing good. That is, he just happened to be standing next to an empty car at the very moment his sister needed one.

"Hell's bells," Merle heard his sister say.

"What's wrong," he asked, "are you OK?"

"Oh, I'm fine, but I'm afraid we've got a problem."

"What's that?" he asked.

"I didn't leave room for my bees."

"What do you mean room for your bees?" Merle said, thinking he'd misunderstood.

"Just that," Sara Jean said impatiently, as she prodded the tightly packed boxes in her car. "I'm filled to the gills, and there's no room left for my bees." She threw up her hands in exasperation.

As for Merle, he was immediately lost in a terrifying Halloween movie plot, in which someone (him) was waking up in the backseat of a car, hands and feet duct-taped to a beehive full of Africanized killer bees, a timer ticking away that would at any moment unleash a deadly swarm.

"Merle," Sara Jean said. "Merle!" Sara Jean said again, the second time loud enough to startle him.

"Oh, sorry," he said. "I thought for a second you said you intended to put a beehive in your car."

"That's what I said," Sara Jean replied. "At least that was my original plan, but as you can see that's not happening."

She noted the horrified look on her brother's face.

"I know you think it's crazy, Merle," Sara Jean said, "but it's perfectly safe because the bees are sealed inside. There's no chance of even one escaping. It's no different than carrying a box of books or a hamster in a cage."

"I beg to disagree," Merle said, a bit more forcefully than he had intended, "but in my estimation there's a world of difference between hamsters, books, and bees. Never heard of anyone being attacked by a swarm of hamsters or copies of *The Great Gatsby*!"

Why Merle and Sara Jean didn't just swap cars remains an unaddressed question. However, family members speculated after the fact that Sara Jean may have thought there was therapeutic value in making Merle face his fears. But motivation hardly matters because Merle agreed despite his initial reservations, a reluctance that was ameliorated somewhat as he watched Sara Jean vigorously jiggle the hive's locked entrance door.

"You see?" she said. "Nothing scary about it. Just a wood box. I'll throw a bedsheet over it if that would make you feel better."

"Small comfort," Merle said through the mesh of an old bee hat Sara Jean had given him to ease his fears as he stood next to the hive, "but all right. You've convinced me, although you know better than anyone how I feel about bees. I think I'd rather face down a wild boar than a bee—damn embarrassing thing to admit."

"I do understand, Merle," Sara Jean said empathetically, "but you don't have to worry. Besides," she said with a mischievous smile, "my bees are safer to have in your car than a wild boar. I'm sure of that."

"I'm gonna have to trust you on that, sis," Merle said with a slight, hopeful smile.

Thinking back on it, Sara Jean should have ended their conversation on that positive note. But she and Merle had a history of playful banter, so this seemed a good time to add a few points to that scoreboard.

"Just make sure you don't have an accident," she said, "and if you do, I'd suggest you get out fast and shut the door behind you."

It was a joke that Merle didn't find useful or humorous, but he chuckled along with his sister anyway.

Merle interlocked his car's backseat safety belts and roped them around the hive to hold it down and then draped a white bedsheet that Sara Jean had given him over it. From the outside the covered hive looked more like an overweight Casper the Friendly Ghost than anything else. He thought about drawing a happy face on the sheet with a black marker but didn't think Sara Jean would appreciate him ruining her sheet. Still, he chuckled, thinking about what passing motorists might think if they noticed his ghost, and the humor of it helped him tamp down the residual fear of bees that was always inside him.

When he was in college, a large bumblebee interrupted a conversation he was having with his girlfriend, Amelie Dupree, and a group of other classmates on his university's leafy quad. It was a warm spring afternoon, and students were either rushing to their next class with intention on their faces or sitting on one of the quad's substantial granite memorial benches or perhaps lounging on the grass beneath mature oak trees reading a book. Merle was well-liked and considered happy and carefree, so it was surprising—perhaps even shocking—when the lumbering arrival of a single bumblebee caused Merle to nearly levitate, drop his backpack, and run toward the safety of the administration building as if he were being chased by a crazed terrorist. Amelie could do nothing but watch him sprint across the quad, too frozen by confusion and fear to chase after him.

Although he explained why he was so deathly afraid of bees when Amelie later found Merle looking out on the quad from behind the administration building's protective plate glass window, the incident definitely took some of the shine off their relationship; perhaps because Amelie was a biology major who was unafraid of bees or any other insect. His friends, especially the males, ribbed him mercilessly. For weeks after the incident, he couldn't shake the feeling that his classmates, at least those who had witnessed his arms-flailing retreat, took every opportunity to retell the embarrassing story.

Sara Jean told Merle she would take the lead because her new twenty-five-acre farm was in the middle of nowhere and hard to find. It was land Sara Jean intended to use as both a buffer against the creeping suburbanization she hated and as an anchor for her new business selling locally grown produce and honey products to the growing number of farm-to-table restaurants in Raleigh.

"Merle, why don't you follow me since I know where I'm going?" she said. "My farm's hard to find unless you've been there before."

He smiled, seeing a sparring opportunity.

"That's fine," he said, "but if your farm is that hard to find, how are your customers going to find you?"

"Oh, they won't have any trouble once I put up my signs," she said, slightly annoyed, "but right now that's low on my priority list. You just take care of my bees. They're gonna make liquid gold for me."

"Don't worry," he said, "me and your bees will get along just fine." He hoped this was true, but frankly he was still convincing himself as he glanced out at his sideview mirror and watched Sara Jean's former gravel driveway disappear behind him like a mirage.

The first part of the trip was uneventful, just a short drive down the interstate before he followed Sara Jean onto a sparsely traveled secondary road, a scenic route that would allow for slow and careful driving. Disappointingly, Merle's ghostly passenger went unnoticed while they were on the interstate, at least as far as Merle could tell. Once they were on the secondary road, Merle turned up the radio volume and avoided glancing up at his rearview mirror. It was a simple avoidance strategy to help him forget the fact that thousands of the tiny creatures that had once conspired to kill him were trapped in a wooden box under a bedsheet in his backseat.

His other avoidance technique was focusing on the radiant, cloudless, dark blue sky framed by his car's windshield, something that allowed Merle to indulge in a long overdue bout of nostalgia as he thought about his life in general and about this road in particular. It was a sparsely traveled route he had taken many times on his way home from college, mostly on holidays and sometimes during spring and summer breaks. He smiled thinking about the overwhelming sense of optimism he'd felt back then.

In those days he had driven a rusted-out MG that only an engineering student could keep running. Although he mostly traveled the road by himself, he'd occasionally made the trip with Amelie. He recalled how much he loved the car, especially when Amelie was in the passenger seat, her hair tied up with a long scarf, and how he liked watching the ends of her hair dance erotically in the slipstream behind her. He always thought she looked like a young Audrey Hepburn.

He had loved college, especially after meeting Amelie at the beginning of his sophomore year. He had done well enough in his engineering studies but took a semester off his junior year because he was on the pay-as-you-go college plan. He got a summer job with an electrical contracting company that paid him handsomely and had he not reconnected with his high school girlfriend LeeAnn Price he might have returned to college to finish his degree.

Even now he sometimes mused about his life and how it might have turned out differently had Amelie not broken up with him (something she claimed had nothing to do with the bumblebee incident). Perhaps if he had seen a therapist at the time and had not dropped out of school his life would have taken a different path than it did. But all that was water under the bridge, as the saying goes.

As it was, the twin siren calls of love and money had derailed his higher education plans quicker than he could have imagined. Still, he had no regrets about his choice. He'd lived a reasonably happy life after marrying LeeAnn, who was pretty enough to be the homecoming queen of his high school class, smart enough to be the office manager for the largest real estate company in town, and strong enough to be an adored mother to their three children. And she was still someone who deeply loved and appreciated Merle Flack for many reasons including his good and tender heart.

How Merle could have missed seeing the massive tractor pull into his lane from a freshly tilled field is still a mystery to everyone except Merle. He knew exactly why the accident happened. He had been daydreaming about Amelie. Specifically, he had been daydreaming about the days when he and Amelie skipped class to meet in his dorm room on sultry, hot afternoons. He could still conjure up the musty, sweet smells that their lovemaking left in the room, a powerful and erotic scent that he hoped would still be there when he returned from his last class of the day.

This familiar stretch of road also held its own intoxicating and perhaps even more distracting expression of his youthful libido. Principally, it was the memory of how he and Amelie had gotten caught in a sudden summer rainstorm while driving home on this same road and how he had sought shelter in a nearby patch of woods that separated two soybean fields. It was too good of an opportunity to pass up, something that Amelie clearly understood when she bounded over the low-slung car door and stood with her hands raised to the sky laughing hysterically as she repeated something in French over and over. Merle didn't understand any French, but he got the drift of what she was saying when she pulled her summer dress over her head and threw it in his direction.

"Now we do not have to worry about getting our clothes wet," she had said, giving him a look that didn't need translation. Just the thought of that afternoon could still cause his heart to race (if he ever allowed himself to think about it), especially when he imagined the feel of their naked, rain-soaked bodies pressed up against the still warm hood of his beloved MG. Unfortunately, this was an inopportune time for these highly distracting daydreams.

Sara Jean, of course, did not know that Merle would use his driving time to reminisce about having sex with his college girlfriend to the point of distraction. Otherwise, her assumptions about the route were spot on. Only a few cars stacked up behind them as they sliced through vast tracts of agricultural land planted with soybeans, corn, and other reliable cash crops, and she was right about Merle getting used to her bees. In fact, right up until the moment his path was blocked by an enormous tractor, Merle truly believed he was carrying nothing more frightening than a box of happy hamsters.

Thankfully, Merle was barely exceeding forty miles an hour when he reflexively slammed on the brakes in a desperate attempt to avoid the accident. He immediately felt his car begin a slow, rearward spin. For most people this would have been a time to panic, especially after the car's left rear wheel lost contact with the pavement. But Merle was not known for panicking about anything (except for bees, of course).

He turned his steering wheel into the spin and was relieved when his car's back wheels grabbed the road just seconds before he heard the sickening sound of his car's rear bumper smash into the tractor's enormous, dirt-encrusted tire. The impact, and his head slamming into the car's headrest, woke Merle up to two essential realities: one, he was never going to see, much less have sex with, Amelie again; and two, he had a box full of angry bees in his backseat.

He glanced over his shoulder in a panic and saw Sara Jean's sheet in a bundle on the car's floorboard, but he was relieved to see the hive still sitting upright. He blew out a lungful of nervously held air and relaxed as he waited for the car to spin out its kinetic energy. When the car came to rest on the road's narrow shoulder, he was facing the calming sight of a dense, green cornfield. He was just about to thank God for delivering him without injury when he noticed a bee perched strategically on his rearview mirror like the advance scout of an invading army. "Oh, shit," he said, as he fumbled with his seat belt. "Holy shit!"

Sara Jean had witnessed none of this horrifying incident, even in her rearview mirror, because she was preoccupied with thinking through her business plan and potential naming options for her honey products. Had she been paying attention to how closely Merle was following her, she would have seen a kelly green tractor pull out of the cornfield right into the path of her brother's car. Then, had she pulled off the road to deal with that traumatic experience, she would have witnessed an even more distressing sight. Merle, her beloved brother, sprinting down the road's shimmering blacktop in her direction, his arms swinging wildly as he disappeared like a frightened animal into the neatly aligned rows of cornstalks.

As it was, Sara Jean was completely focused on her business ideas at the exact moment Merle was spastically fumbling like a cartoon character to free himself from the encumbering airbags that pressed against him, now as limp and deflated as his overwrought Amelie fantasies.

And while the cabin of Sara Jean's car was calm and subdued, Merle was trapped inside a full-fledged nightmare, one made even more terrifying by the thousands of agitated bees who now joined together to create a cacophony of saw-singing, atonal sounds that reminded him of 1950s science fiction movies where giant ants or praying mantises swooped down from the sky to eat unsuspecting motorists.

Had Merle been someone with a healthy respect for bees rather than someone traumatized into a deathly fear of them, he might have taken a moment to assess the situation and quickly determine how many bees had escaped, beyond the one still resting on his rearview mirror, before making his next move. As it was, Merle just assumed the worst and bolted, rocketed really, out from under his car's steering wheel and ran for his life, first down the blacktop, and then into what he thought was the safety of a six-foot high row of cornstalks.

The driver of the tractor, Willy White, had a catbird seat from which to observe both the accident and Merle's unhinged dash for his life. From his perspective, watching Merle's late model Ford sedan spin like a top into his brand-new tractor was like watching a movie from the comfort of his La-Z-Boy recliner at home where the consequences of what he witnessed were someone else's job to clean up. Maybe that's why he managed a quick chuckle as he watched Merle flee the scene as if he were on fire. It was a scene so surreal that he half expected to hear a director yell, "Cut" and see a full-on film crew rush onto the deserted blacktop to block out the next shot.

Willy didn't mention any of these imaginings to the police officer who eventually showed up to investigate the accident. By then Willy's feet were firmly planted in reality, and he was more concerned about the time he was wasting and the damage Merle might have done to his tractor. However, it was plain to see that Merle's Ford, with its accordioned trunk and folded-back tires, was the clear loser of the competition.

"Yep, never seen anything like it," Willy told the investigating officer, who himself looked like he had just walked off a movie set with his signature shaved head partially covered by a stiff platelike hat cocked at a jaunty angle and his eyes covered by impenetrable mirrored sunglasses resting just so on the bridge of his nose. "That fellow over there," Willy continued, pointing at Merle who was now leaning against Sara Jean's car after he'd found his way out of the cornfield, "well, he just flew out of his car like a lunatic. I do hope he's all right. You don't think he's on drugs or something?"

"Nope, don't think so," the officer replied without emotion or judgment. "It seems he was carrying a beehive in the backseat, and he got a bit distracted by it."

Willy looked incredulously at the officer. "What do you mean, a beehive in his backseat?" he said. "Who carries a beehive in their car, especially if they're that afraid of bees?"

"My question exactly," the officer said flatly, as if he were delivering a line in Willy's mental movie. "You are not wrong about that."

A few weeks later, after Sara Jean and the rest of her family had moved into the new house and Merle had settled with his insurance company and bought a new car, Merle visited his sister. He brought along one of LeeAnn's sought-after pound cakes. They shared a piece sitting out on Sara Jean's new deck. By this time, Merle and Sara Jean had discussed the accident and its consequences so many times that humor had begun to seep into their conversations about it.

"So, you still like your new car?" Sara Jean asked, putting down her empty plate and fork on the coffee table between them and picking up her coffee mug.

"I do," Merle said, taking a last bite of cake, "although I might have chosen a different path to replacing it." He chuckled as he picked up his own coffee cup.

"I'll say," Sara Jean replied. "Still, I'm sorry you had to go through all that."

"Oh, it's all right," he said, "I probably should have been paying more attention to the road."

Sara Jean let that revelation sit a few beats before following up on it. "Well, now that you mention it," she said, settling back into her chair, "I would really like to know what you were thinking about that day. How could you miss seeing something as huge as a green tractor pull in front of you on that deserted road? Did my bees distract you that much?"

Merle thought a moment before he answered. He and his sister had a history of honesty between them, so he thought this was a good time to come clean.

"Well, to tell the truth, Sara Jean," Merle said in a confessional tone of voice, "I was neck deep in my own thoughts, and I can assure you I wasn't thinking about bees."

"Oh, really. So, what were you thinking about?" Sara Jean asked with new interest.

"It's embarrassing to say," Merle admitted.

"Come on, you can tell me, Merle," she coaxed. "Besides, I'm your sister and I already know all your secrets," she said, digging for details as she'd done when they were in high school and reluctantly revealed secrets about their current love interests to each other.

Merle considered her argument for candor, then sheepishly confessed, "All right, but you can't laugh. I was thinking about Amelie Dupree."

Sara Jean almost spit out her last sip of coffee. "Don't tell me you're still carrying a torch for your French girlfriend," she said, barely able to contain her glee. "I admit she was beautiful and exotic and sexy, but that was more than twenty-five years ago, Merle. At some point, you've got to let it go."

"I know," Merle agreed, "but for some reason she keeps popping up. Maybe it's a man thing. I really loved her, and God, you just don't know."

"Oh, please," Sara Jean said, "spare me. Besides, Amelie would no more have married you and moved to Greenwood than she'd have she'd have married you and moved to the North Pole."

"Yep, you're probably right about that," Merle said, closing his eyes to conjure up Amelie's immutable twenty-one-year-old face. "Still, talk about precious memories. I sometimes . . ."

"That'll do," Sara Jean said. "I know exactly why you ran into that farmer's tractor. Jesus, you guys are so predictable."

Sara Jean got up and walked toward the edge of her expansive deck. "So, you want to see where I put my beehive?" she asked, pointing to a clearing about a hundred yards away. "You can keep your distance this time. No beekeeper equipment needed."

"I appreciate that," Merle said, standing up and walking toward her. Sara Jean hooked her arm around Merle's arm when they met at the deck's edge, and they walked arm in arm down the stairs and onto a well-maintained lawn that felt like a padded carpet under their feet.

Sara Jean was known for saying what she thought, so Merle was not surprised when she resurfaced their Amelie conversation.

"But seriously, Merle," Sara Jean said, placing her hand on his, "if you ask me, all this daydreaming about Amelie makes me think you're more afraid of your fast-approaching middle age than you are of my bees." She offered a sisterly, compassionate smile.

"So, you're a philosopher now, Sara Jean," Merle said, slightly irritated, although he knew she was right. "Maybe you should sell your homespun wisdom along with your honey."

"I'll admit I'm no philosopher," she replied, "but you know me, I say what I think."

"Yeah, I know."

"But now that you mention it," Sara Lee continued, "that's not a bad idea. Maybe put a little nugget of wisdom on every jar of honey—sort of like a fortune cookie—that's a great idea."

"Yeah, well, sorry I mentioned it," Merle said.

Merle watched from a distance while Sara Jean tended to her bees. He thought about her advice and the wisdom of it, about the choices he'd made in life and their consequences, about his successes and failures, about his happy marriage and healthy children. He had a lot to be thankful for, he concluded. Still, he couldn't think of any good reason to completely jettison the memory of Amelie, even if that were possible.

It really is a guy thing, he thought, something his sister, and certainly not LeeAnn, would never understand. And with that, he took one last vivid daydreaming trip (at least for now) to a long-disappeared dorm room in the spring of his youth. Then he looked up at the bright, iridescent blue sky and smiled.

6

Valerie Jean Smith

MARY LOUISE MCADAMS AND VALERIE JEAN SMITH had known each other their entire lives, but they hadn't exactly been friends—a fact that Mary Louise's mother often cited as a good example of her daughter's moral turpitude.

However, all that changed one day after algebra class when Valerie Jean pinned Mary Louise against her hall locker and proceeded to overwhelm her with a torrent of words and enthusiasm, two of the three things she was known for, the third being her own lack of moral turpitude.

"Mary Louise, I need to ask you a favor," she began. "You might not know it, but I've always envied your math skills. Me, I'd swear Mrs. Johnson is speaking in tongues. Holy Jesus! Like today, I didn't understand a thing. Did you? Of course, you did. You always seem to get it, but I can't afford to be lost because I need good math grades to get into medical school. I bet you never feel that way—lost, I mean—you're like a math genius, right?"

Valerie Jean took a breath, and Mary Louise thought about responding, but she wasn't sure what to say. The thing is, when Valerie Jean started talking, and it didn't matter whether she was talking about shopping for a new pair of shoes or a date she'd had, it was best to just wait it out, like being caught on a porch during a sudden summer rain shower.

Frankly, Mary Louise was not surprised Valerie Jean was having a hard time with math. Before getting to know her, she had often wondered what Valerie Jean was doing in advanced placement classes in the first place because she assumed, like everyone else at Greenwood High School, that all Valerie Jean was interested in was honing her wild child reputation.

"You give me too much credit, Valerie," Mary Louise said. "I'm no genius, and besides the only reason I'm good at math is because my mom sends me to math and science camps every summer."

She immediately felt stupid for mentioning math camp.

"You're too funny," Valerie Jean said, "but compared to me you really are a math whiz, so I'd say math camp was a good idea. So, what do you think? Should I come over after school? Does that work for you?"

"Sure," Mary Louise answered, reflexively, like someone tied to a straight-backed chair in an abandoned warehouse trying to avoid a beating, except instead of fear, Mary Louise felt nothing but exhilaration and joy. Valerie Jean Smith, one of the school's most popular and dangerous girls (at least according to most of the school's mothers) was asking for her help, an ask that held out the possibility they might become friends. Mary Louise was over the moon.

In high school, Valerie Jean's overwhelming power of persuasion was "just Valerie's way." She showed up, started talking, often flitting from one topic to the next like a frenetic bee buzzing among bee balm blossoms. And even if the narrative she spun was hard to follow, the point she made, for the most part, was salient, entertaining, and occasionally profound.

Still, Valerie Jean's sales-like powers of persuasion could be reputationally dangerous, so the one thing Mary Louise learned early on in their friendship was to avoid conversational fillers like "sure" and "absolutely." Too much of that, and she might find herself driving down an old logging road on a warm summer night toward a secluded cove at Lake Greenwood and swimming naked and free in the cool water, darting in and out of the headlights like beautiful, shimmering fish irresistibly drawn to the golden light.

Mary Louise's mother was clear about what she thought of Valerie Jean's proposed visit, which was a disappointing but unsurprising response, Mary Louise concluded.

"Mary Louise Anne Marie McAdams," she said, "I don't believe for a minute that Valerie has the slightest interest in studying. Really, I don't mean to be unchristian, but as far as I can tell, the only subjects Valerie focuses on are boys and drinking."

"Mom," Mary Louise shrieked. "That's not true! You don't even know her! And besides most of that gossip about boys and drinking isn't even true."

"And how would you know?" her mother replied with a good measure of parental incredulity.

Her mother did have a point. Mary Louise didn't know much about Valerie Jean other than she was the most envied, despised, condemned, and praised girl at school. She was also the most beautiful, someone who wore her extraordinary gifts of chiseled but voluptuous proportions like everyone else wears a comfortable pair of jeans: unassuming and without thought.

"Look, Mary Louise," her mother said in the calm, authoritative voice that always infuriated her. "You're right, I don't know if what I've heard about Valerie Jean is true, but I will tell you this, if you lie down with dogs, don't be surprised if you wake up with fleas. So, here's a fact you can bank on, being friends with Valerie Jean Smith will lead to nothing but trouble."

It was easy to understand why Mary Louise's mom and the other members of the town's professional class of busybodies thought Valerie Jean was an evil pied piper sent to lead their children off toward ruination and disgrace. She dressed as she pleased and dated and had sex with whomever she pleased (or so everyone thought), all without the slightest bit of regret or shame. Valerie Jean was truly a liberated woman, someone her friends might have judged a small-town version of Simone de Beauvoir or Collette, had they known about the famous French libertines. As it was, everyone was just in awe of how Valerie Jean seemed to move through life with such abandonment, freedom, and curiosity.

It was this combination of joie de vivre that attracted just about every male in town like ants to an overturned Coke bottle left on a picnic table. In fact, one of the town's most respected bankers, Mr. Fine, once drove into a lamppost while watching Valerie walk down Main Street wearing a skirt of nearly transparent silk that floated around her waist like a gossamer cloud.

Back then, Valerie Jean had seemed oblivious to her impact on men or how she tied them up in Gordian knots of sexual fantasy, denial, and ultimately disgust with themselves for having such thoughts in the first place. Years later, on a drive with Mary Louise from Greenwood to Atlanta where she was doing her dermatology residency, she confessed that a good part of her younger persona had been a middle-finger salute to the assumptions that everyone made about her.

"We've been friends for a long time, ML, so you remember how people were back then. They could be downright cruel, but I was determined not to be cowed. I did as I pleased, not so much to make a point—that would be letting them win—but because I felt no need to hide the real me. If they didn't like it, that was their problem. But every now and then," she admitted, revealing her often hidden emotions, "it really, really hurt, you know."

"Yes, I imagine it did," Mary Louise said, empathizing with the pain her friend felt as someone unfairly judged. At the same time, she found herself fighting a tide of less empathetic feelings, specifically her own jealousy that Valerie Jean was both drop-dead gorgeous and maddeningly, more organically intelligent than she would ever be.

"I guess that explains why I pushed boundaries, you know," Valerie Jean said, "to really give them something to talk about." A slight smile formed at the corners of her mouth as she peered over her sunglasses at Mary Louise. Then, she broke out in a full-throated belly laugh. Mary Louise joined in because she knew exactly what boundary-pushing example of poor judgment Valerie Jean was referring to, something Mary Louise's mother still called "the incident," irrespective of her daughter's many other redemptive accomplishments.

To be fair, the circumstances of the incident were innocent enough. First, the idea of using Aaron McAfee's Porsche convertible—he was Valerie Jean's boyfriend at the time—for a day trip to the beach would never have come up had he not told Valerie Jean that the bright red sports car was a gift from his father, Swanson McAfee, one of most successful attorneys in the state.

Second, the incident happened in the spring of their senior year, and the girls both had a legitimate reason—studying for their final exams—to beg off from family outings. Mary Louise's parents were visiting her grandparents up in Raleigh, and Valerie Jean's family had rented a retreat cabin in the mountains near Asheville.

And third, taking a road trip to the beach, even without their parents' permission, was not really unreasonable given that Mary Louise was the class valedictorian and Valerie Jean, with Mary Louise's math help, was graduating near the top of their class. They both believed they had earned some slack.

The plan for the day was clean and simple. They'd pack bathing suits, a change of clothes, and a picnic basket. They'd drive to Atlantic Beach or Wrightsville Beach, tan, flirt, make unkept promises to everyone, and then come home with a good story to tell. What could possibly go wrong?

Unfortunately, what they didn't know about Mr. McAfee was that despite his success, the idea of giving his son a sports car would have bent him over in a fit of laughter. His children had never been handed anything and were expected to work for everything they had. If Aaron had a car to offer it would have been a serviceable, high-mileage Ford—not a shiny new Porsche—and if he had one, he would have bought it with money he'd earned on his own.

"Valerie, are you sure it's OK to borrow Aaron's car?" Mary Louise asked as they drove to Aaron's house in her mom's boat-like station wagon.

"Oh, absolutely," Valerie Jean said confidently. "Aaron showed me just last week where to find the garage door key—under a flowerpot—and the spare car key—in an old dresser drawer. And he said that I could absolutely borrow the car if I ever needed one. So here we are, needing one, and it's just the right car for an impromptu trip to the beach."

"I'm not so sure," May Louise said, a lot less confidently. "Why don't we just take this car?"

"Mary Louise, you're such a Debbie Downer," Valerie Jean scolded. "Are you saying you'd rather drive your mother's houseboat to the beach? Seriously, what kind of story is that? 'So, we took my mother's station wagon, a six-pack of Cokes, some peanut butter sandwiches, and off we went!' That's embarrassing, nothing like a story that begins, 'So, we borrowed a friend's Porsche, raided our parents' liquor cabinet, drove to the beach, and spent the day tanning and flirting."

"That IS a better story," Mary Louise admitted, "except for the part you left out: the part that ends with and then they carted us off to jail!"

"Good God," Valerie Jean said with frustration in her voice, which was the tone she always took back then when Mary Louise challenged her most outlandish ideas, before life and experience installed a curb on her excessive enthusiasm, "will you just relax and live a little?"

Valerie Jean had offered Mary Louise this live-your-life-and-relax counsel many times during their young friendship. Like the day at Lake Greenwood when Mary Louise refused to smoke pot while they sunbathed on the bow of Valerie Jean's family ski boat. And then later when she refused to lose her bikini top, even though she knew no one would see them.

Eventually, Mary Louise had been convinced by this live-your-life shaming, and she did smoke Valerie Jean's pot and later enthusiastically joined in when Valerie Jean suggested they skinny-dip in the lake's cool, refreshing water. The abandonment of established convention turned an ordinary day at the lake into one of the most magical and memorable afternoons of Mary Louise's young life.

Valerie Jean had also given Mary Louise this advice when she was considering having sex with her first real boyfriend, Bradley McConaughey, the summer of her junior year. Bradley was another academically smart kid who excelled at football and baseball and had a well-deserved reputation for being a decent, respectful, and unassuming young man.

Mary Louise and Bradley had known each other since kindergarten and had even performed together two years running in the annual Greenwood Baptist Church nativity pageant. Bradley always got a speaking part welcoming Jesus to the world. Mary Louise played one of the Christmas trees in the background, her costume being a cardboard facsimile of a Christmas tree that she held up in front of her. She had made the tree herself and had covered it as instructed with green and silver glitter. The covering made her tree sparkle in the white-hot glare of a spotlight, and she made swishing sounds when the choir director waved her hands in Mary Louise's direction.

It was not that she saw anything wrong with sex despite her mom's age-old admonition about not needing to buy the cow when the milk was free. It was just that she didn't want anything to go wrong. Mary Louise did then—and still does—carry around a near-pathological need to dither and ruminate before making most decisions. It was this tendency that drove Valerie Jean to distraction because she often acted first and only checked later for potential consequences. This personality dynamic between them, the yin and yang of unchecked abandonment and overwrought reserve, was exactly what made their friendship so successful. Unfortunately, at the time of the car-borrowing incident, excess won the day.

Valerie found the garage key just where Aaron said it would be, underneath a small flowerpot next to the garage door. The car key was also in the top drawer of an old dresser pushed against the back wall of the family's cavernous three-car garage. Mary Louise stood outside the garage door and held it open as if refusing to cross the threshold might somehow absolve her from a future charge of breaking and entering.

"Here's the key," Valerie yelled when she found it, her voice echoing in the absence of the family's two other cars. Mrs. McAfee's car was out getting new tires, and the family-size station wagon was transporting the McAfee family to Charlottesville for a tour of the University of Virginia where Aaron planned to go to college.

"Open the garage door, ML," Valerie Jean commanded, pointing to a switch just inside the door on the wall. "Come on," she said, "this is going to be so much fun. You'll see."

Mary Louise didn't respond as she hesitantly flicked the garage door switch and watched the door's tiny aluminum wheels rattle and clank as the door creeped along a more substantial-looking guide rail. It was a sound at the time that seemed ominous and foreboding and entirely too loud for its purpose. Valerie Jean ignored her friend's reluctance, convinced that Mary Louise would come around once they were out on the open road and watching the trailing edges of each other's hair dance a jig like one of those attention-grabbing, tube men that car dealerships used along the highway to draw attention.

It took Valerie a few tries to find the reverse gear, but once she found it, she clearly knew how to baby the clutch just enough to ease the rumbling, beautiful machine out of the garage and into the blinding light of a glorious spring morning. Then, with the car still running, Valerie Jean pulled the handbrake and extricated herself from behind the wheel to sit on the doorframe.

"Wanna get that garage door, ML?" she said, hiking up her skirt and posing like a model from one of those misogynistic calendars that service stations used to hang behind their service counters featuring bikini-clad models straddling a shiny new set of tires or lovingly stroking oversize chrome exhaust pipes.

Once they'd left the Greenwood city limits, Mary Louise relaxed enough to let Valerie Jean crank up the radio. Until then, Mary Louise had been as nervous as a cat and insisted that Valerie Jean obey the posted speed limit signs so they wouldn't draw too much attention. This advice meant Valerie Jean hardly ever shifted out of first gear, something that attracted *more* attention, not less.

One of the reasons they settled on Atlantic Beach was because getting lost on the way was impossible. Any one of a half-dozen roads out of Greenwood would eventually get them to Route 70, which offered a clear path east to the beach. Even if they got lost, there were plenty of road signs. Still, Mary Louise insisted on bringing a road map, something that Valerie Jean complained just diminished the potential adventure of getting lost.

"How did you learn to drive a manual shift?" Mary Louise asked once they'd left town and were driving to speed.

"That's easy," Valerie said as she expertly downshifted through the gears to slow for a stop sign. "My grandfather had a farm, and he let me drive his old Ford pickup, even though I was only fourteen at the time. He had learned young, so he said I should too. At first, I drove around the farm and then on country roads. Eventually, Pops sent me on errands in town even though I didn't even have my learner's permit at the time."

"That's wild," Mary Louise said, "but an old truck is different from a sports car."

"You're right about that," Valerie Jean said. "That's why I made Aaron let me drive on the few occasions we used his car on dates, although he whined the whole time about being careful. He was forever telling me to watch out for this and that, to slow down and speed up—drove me insane so I mostly ignored him."

It took about twenty minutes for Mary Louise and Valerie Jean to cover the distance between Greenwood and Route 70. By the time the car merged onto the road, Mary Louise was no longer anxious, and that emotion was as distant as a childhood memory. She was now fully committed to trusting Valerie Jean's instincts and her vision of an orderly, insistent universe where things went mostly to plan. Mary Louise smiled in Valerie Jean's direction in a way that let her know she was all in, then they both put on their sunglasses and turned to face the empty road that stretched endlessly before them.

※

The landscape in the eastern part of North Carolina, especially down toward the coast, is mostly farmland planted with corn, soybeans, and cash crops of one variety or another. As such, there's not much other scenery to break up the ride in the spring except gas stations; old farmhouses; and empty, weathered, makeshift vegetable stands waiting in anticipation of the next harvest season.

Dozens of small cinder-block churches also accented the landscape, many with teetering, haphazardly constructed steeples. The denomination of the churches, serving pastors, and upcoming sermons were displayed under glass-covered placards that faced the road. Some of the church names were straightforward like Christ the Redeemer Reformed Church, while other congregations adopted names that left no room for ambiguity: Resurrection and Light, Holy Redeemer, Jesus Christ of Nazareth Church.

The girls had been driving less than an hour, mostly in silence because road noise made conversation impossible, when Mary Louise noticed that the car's gas indicator was dangerously close to empty, something that provoked her own anxiety, but barely registered with Valerie Jean even when she mentioned it to her.

"We should get some gas," Mary Louise said, trying to keep the worry out of her voice. Valerie Jean glanced down at the indicator. "Yep, should do that soon," she said without much concern. "I think we're a long way from running out."

"OK," Mary Louise said agreeably, but then added, "still, I need to pee so I'd appreciate it if we could stop soon." Truthfully, Mary Louise could have easily made it to the beach, but old habits like excessive anxiety die hard.

A few miles farther on, Valerie pulled off the road and drove toward a squat, sad-looking building with a few rusted gas pumps out front. A large oval sign hung over the entrance that announced the girls had arrived at Jake's Country Store. Its market specialty, "Good Food, Cheap Gas," was highlighted in blue and red lettering, recently touched up. The sign was positioned underneath the station's faded namesake, which had once been outlined by neon tubing but now only the support stubs remained.

Valerie pulled up to one of the two rusty pumps and turned off the engine. The gas station attendant, a decent-looking, shaggy-haired boy wearing a Grateful Dead T-shirt underneath an unbuttoned faded denim work shirt and wearing a pair of ripped jeans, was sitting in one of a dozen weathered straight-backed chairs lined up along an elevated concrete apron that wrapped around the building.

The attendant hitched up his jeans and smoothed his work shirt as he walked toward the car. Mary Louise expected him to do what most men did in Valerie's presence: fall all over themselves to impress her. This attendant was different. He veered off toward the front of the car without making eye contact. Then he shook his head and pursed his lips enough to blow out a low, birdlike whistling sound.

"Woo-eee, that is one nice car," he said as he stalked around the car like a cat on a hunt. He ignored Mary Louise and Valerie Jean as if they were just two lifelike mannequins in halter tops and short skirts sitting low and exposed on the Porsche's black leather seats. Mary Louise found the inattention personally disappointing.

"I appreciate it, Carlton," Valerie Jean said, squinting to find his name stitched in white thread on his work shirt. "It's my boyfriend's car," she continued, "but he let us borrow it. Do you like cars? Frankly, I don't know much about them. In fact, I'm not sure what kind of gas to use. Could you help me with that? We'd be grateful if you could."

"Sure," Carlton said, smiling and clearly enjoying his car knowledge advantage. "I was just reading about this car yesterday in a magazine. Porsche nine eleven, right?"

"That's right. You do know your cars," Valerie Jean said with a Blanche Dubois tone she sometimes took with men, mostly for the fun of it since she really didn't need to play that game to get along in the world. After that, Carlton fell willingly under her spell. She knew she could get him to do anything: gas up the car, check the tire pressure, change the windshield wipers, or even spot polish the car as if it were sitting in his own driveway.

While Carlton serviced the car, Valerie Jean and Mary Louise used the restroom at the back of the building, which was less disgusting than they expected. Later they put sodas and chips on the counter in front of Carlton's cash register and sat outside in two of the less rickety chairs to watch Carlton work.

"He's really enjoying himself," Mary Louise said to Valerie Jean, with just a bit of cattiness.

"Seems to be," Valerie Jean said, "but I really wasn't sure about what kind of gas to get. I'm glad Carlton's on it."

"He's kinda cute, don't you think?" Mary Louise said.

"He is, now that you mention it," Valerie Jean agreed.

"You want to take Carlton with us?" she continued.

"Should we?"

"If you want, but I think you can do better."

"Yeah, guess you're right," Mary Louise said, pretending to be a pro at this. "Plus, as a general rule it's never a good idea to kidnap the first gas station attendant who fills your tank."

"Smart girl," Valerie Jean said, cocking her head and raising an eyebrow. "It's no wonder you're our class valedictorian."

Once they were back on the road and the whining noises churning up from the road made it impossible to talk, Mary Louise thought about how they'd flirted shamelessly with Carlton. She felt a little guilty about leaving him standing next to the station's rusted gas pumps, waving enthusiastically as they drove away. His face had the same confused look people get after they've handed over all their money to a street hustler in a game of three-cup switcheroo and still can't for the life of them figure out what went wrong.

They hadn't really conned Carlton. He had seemed genuinely happy to gas up the girls' car and clean their windshield to a gleaming, spotless shine. Still, it didn't seem right to Mary Louise, although they'd likely made his day and gave him a good story to tell his buddies.

Carlton had helped Mary Louise and Valerie Jean repack their cooler with fresh ice, which they had filled with ham sandwiches, sodas, and other picnic supplies. He had also given them useful advice on how to sneak margaritas onto a public beach, the essential ingredient of which, tequila, they had stolen from Valerie Jean's dad's liquor cabinet (aka the sin closet). Valerie Jean's parents were adoptive Southern Baptists—that is, they had been born and saved north of the Mason-Dixon Line—which gave them special dispensation to drink in moderation as long as they didn't mention it to anyone.

"I hope you girls have fun," Carlton had said as he closed Mary Louise's door and stepped away from the car.

"We will," they said in unison, a bit too giggly they both thought, "and when we have our picnic we'll think of you," Mary Louise added with a particularly flirty air. Encouraged by this, Carlton told them to stop by the station on their way home. He clearly knew this was a long shot, but the girls gave him credit for offering.

"And do take care of this beautiful car," he added when Valerie Jean started the engine. "Make sure you wipe it down when you get home. Salt's really bad for a car like this."

"I'll be sure to do that, Carlton," Valerie Jean said as she engaged the clutch and inched off the pump's concrete pad and onto the surrounding pea gravel. Carlton offered some final parting words, but they were muffled by the grinding and crushing sounds the car's tires made as it moved away from the station and back toward Route 70.

※

"There it is! Look, Mary Louise!"

Valerie Jean seemed beside herself as she tried to shake Mary Louise awake so she could see the Atlantic Ocean, patches of which appeared and disappeared in brilliant flashes of light delivered like subliminal messages between the weathered, clapboard beach houses that lined the east side of the road.

Mary Louise had fallen asleep soon after they'd left Carlton, lulled to sleep by the engine's steady vibration and by the blurry greening landscape that whizzed by like an out-of-control diorama. It was a slumber so deep that she was surprised to find herself in the car with Valerie Jean, as if the past few hours had been the most vivid dream she'd ever had.

"What is it? What happened?" Mary Louise asked, pulling herself up in the seat and wiping a streak of drool off her face.

"The Atlantic Ocean!" Valerie screamed, raising her right hand off the gear shift to point toward the ocean.

"Oh, my God, we made it," Mary Louise yelled, truly excited now that she was fully awake.

"What'd I tell you?" Valerie bragged confidently as she shifted up to speed. "We're here, and it's going to be a perfect day. You can stop worrying now."

Atlantic Beach is a barrier island that has been a beach resort since the late 1870s, although not much is left from that time except Fort Macon, a Civil War era relic on the island's northeast side where a few Civil War battles took place in the spring of 1862. Some miles south of Atlantic Beach, the infamous English pirate Blackbeard had run his ship aground, a stolen vessel called *Queen Anne's Revenge*, in June of 1718. As the story goes, Blackbeard had abandoned the stolen ship and survived to pillage the waters between Bermuda and the North Carolina coast until the notorious pirate was killed in November of that same year in an epic battle off the southern tip of Ocracoke, North Carolina.

These historical facts about the notorious pirate, whose real name was Edward Teach, were on the back of a restaurant menu that bore the famous pirate's name. Mary Louise and Valerie Jean stopped at Blackbeard's for coffee after parking the car in a private lot they thought safe from both ogling car enthusiasts and car thieves. Although they were both naïve teenagers, they did know on some level that the car was far from ordinary. But it was Carlton's worship of the car—instead of them—that made them realize Aaron's car must be returned just as they found it: absolutely pristine.

"I do feel better," Mary Louise told Valerie after ordering breakfast. "To tell the truth, I've been worried all along something might happen to Aaron's car."

"It is a sweet car," Valerie agreed, "and now that you mention it, Aaron always seemed nervous when I drove it. I just thought it was a guy thing, always telling me to be careful, like I was too stupid to drive because I'm a girl."

"Well, that's not true," Mary Louise said, trying not to sound too fawning. "You're probably the better driver, although he'd never admit it."

"Yeah," Valerie agreed, "guys can't stand for girls to beat them at anything. That's why they're so predictable, and why beating them at their own game is so easy."

※

Tommy Lee James, or TJ as he was usually known, had serviced Swanson McAfee's cars for years, so picking up his car for service at his house was nothing unusual, even when the family was out of town. What was unusual that day was finding the cavernous garage empty. Swanson never made scheduling mistakes. That's why TJ decided to call Swanson in Charlottesville using the family's garage phone. He had jotted down the hotel's number at the top of the service ticket just in case.

"Hi, Swanson," TJ said without excitement or alarm. "I am in your garage right now, and I'm telling you there ain't no Porsche here. Empty as an old maid's dance card. What do you want me to do?"

Swanson McAfee was known as a cool operator, not someone prone to overreacting, even when his car was missing. He was a methodical thinker in and out of the courtroom, which explained his initial reaction to the news that his car was missing.

"Nothing, right now," Swanson told TJ. "I'll look into it and get back to you."

Looking into it meant questioning his family who were currently waiting in the hotel lobby for him to come down. He had been halfway out the hotel room door when the phone rang, and he answered it only because he thought it was a reminder to hurry up.

"Is something wrong?" his wife June asked when she saw him walking briskly toward them across the well-appointed lobby. He had a concerned look on his face.

"Maybe," he answered as he gathered everyone around him—June, Aaron, and his fifteen-year-old daughter Allison. Then he sat them down on a spacious lobby couch and addressed his family as if they were on a communal witness stand.

"Let me ask you all a question," he said calmly. "Can anyone here think of any reason whatsoever to explain why my car is not in our garage where it belongs?"

They all shook their heads.

"So, are we all agreed to the fact that my red Porsche nine eleven was, in fact, in our garage when we left yesterday?"

Everyone nodded their heads again.

"Are you absolutely sure?" he asked one final time in a lawyerly fashion.

They all nodded, individually and collectively, then responded, "Yes, that is correct," as if they were, in fact, in a courtroom.

"Well, then, in that case," he continued without discernible emotion, "I'd say there definitely is something wrong."

※

After breakfast, Mary Louise and Valerie Jean walked down to the public bathhouse to put on their swimsuits. Mary Louise had brought a sensible one-piece. Valerie Jean had brought a stunningly skimpy bikini, a fashion choice that brought as much admiration and wonder for such a perfect specimen of a human female body as it did envy or lust. They applied generous amounts of sunscreen—at Mary Louise's insistence, of course—and walked down the beach to find an unclaimed patch of sand that looked like it would remain that way for the day. Then, they unfurled two oversize beach blankets, placed just so, two beach chairs, a cooler, two beach bags, and placed two pairs of sandals at their feet and settled in for the day.

"Does it get any better than this?" Valerie Jean asked, throwing her head back to look up at the azure blue sky. She ran both her hands through her long auburn hair.

"No," Mary Louise agreed, "can't see how that's possible."

Although they could not have articulated it at the time, they both knew this to be true, a truth that went beyond simple observation. For a few sweet, uninterrupted hours, they were two teenagers completely in charge of their lives. For Mary Louise, it was a vacation from the relentless need to be perfect—a respite from the worry of making the best grades and full permission to slough off the tyranny of polite, respectful, and chaste behavior and the expectation that she could always be counted on to do the right thing.

For Valerie Jean, it was a vacation from the citizenry of a small

Southern town, who mostly condemned how she conducted her life and expected, even hoped, that she would fail if for no other reason than to prove them right.

Neither one of them would come to these profound realizations about who they were and what motivated them until much later in life. Still, both girls felt a vague sense of relief that day. Here they were, two young girls, their bodies still untouched by time's inevitable cruelty, basking in the hot spring sun, focused on nothing more than ocean waves crashing toward white sand, and the unencumbered, faultless future they still believed stretched out endlessly before them.

"Hey, ML," Valerie Jean said from under her floppy straw hat with a band of small yellow daisies sewn around the brim, "how about some refreshment?"

"You buying?" Mary Louise said, trying to sound sophisticated.

"Yes, I am," Valerie Jean said, as she opened their cooler to retrieve the premixed cocktails they'd made in the parking lot before walking to the beach. This was Carlton's idea, a strategy apparently based on his own experience skirting the rules about drinking on public beaches. He'd also given them plastic cups and straws as his last act of customer service. It made them both think Carlton was a lot smarter than he let on.

"Here's to friends," Valerie Jean said, raising her cup in Mary Louise's direction.

"To best friends," Mary Louise echoed, "and to more days like this."

And that was their day.

Both girls dozed off after finishing their drinks, a deep and satisfying slumber that only hot sand and sun and generously spiked drinks can produce. When they woke up, they ran to the ocean to cool off from the unbearable heat, walked miles along the beach, sometimes arm in arm like old lovers supporting each other, and devoured everything in their cooler. They talked about their plans for college, their boyfriends, and how they hoped their lives would turn out. Some of these hopes became realities: Valerie Jean did become a doctor. Some imaginings—that Mary Louise would be a teacher—did not, although a journalist is not far off the mark.

Valerie Jean and Mary Louise had not discussed their return trip, but when Mary Louise noticed the elongated shadows of people strolling on the beach and the blinding midday light soften and turn a rich hue of yellow and orange, she began crafting a convincing argument for leaving. Not getting caught was at the top of the list. She had read enough books and seen enough movies to know that getting caught in one lie inevitably leads to a second lie, and a third, and a fourth.

She knew her parents would check in after dinner, and if she didn't answer she would be forced into a foundational lie and that lie would lead to another lie until the whole mendacious card stack collapsed. With that unhappy potential in mind, Mary Louise spent the last hour on the beach thinking through every step of their trip home. She created a ten-item, three-hour, mental checklist that would put them at her house just in time to take the inevitable call from her parents. Clearly, there was no time to dillydally, as her mom often said about getting things done.

"Hey, Valerie Jean," Mary Louise said in an unhurried, nonchalant way. "We should probably head back home now."

"What's the rush?" Valerie Jean said. "This is my favorite time of the day. We should stay at least another hour."

"The day did go by fast," Mary Louise agreed, "but if you want to keep our little adventure between you, me, and I suppose Aaron—I'm guessing you do plan to tell him we used his car—then we've got to leave now."

Mary Louise explained the logistics of their return trip and once she did Valerie Jean began packing up without protest. Although she was headstrong, Valerie Jean knew how to listen and could be persuaded by facts and persistence. It was one of the lessons Mary Louise learned from being Valerie Jean's friend, something she later continued to take to work with her every day.

The first four items on Mary Louise's list—leave the beach, shower, dress, and pick up their undamaged, lightly ogled Porsche—were accomplished ahead of schedule. As they drove toward home, Mary Louise checked off each completed waypoint on her schedule and with each checked item she relaxed a little more, like a clock spring moving inextricably away from its breaking point. And so, with the sun still sitting comfortably above the horizon, Mary Louise decided to declare an early victory as she checked off item number six on her mental list: drive home to Greenwood.

She leaned in toward Valerie Jean's ear, shading her eyes from the sun. "We're doing great! What an amazing day," she said. "It's too bad we have to keep this trip a secret." Valerie Jean smiled as she punched the Porsche into cruising gear.

"For now," Valerie Jean said, "for now."

When they passed the exit for Jake's Country Store, Mary Louise considered asking Valerie Jean to stop for gas—item seven—but then thought better of it. Sometimes, the first draft of a story is the best, and the second draft only destroys what was good and true in the original.

The first call that Swanson McAfee made after interrogating his family was to Manny McGregor, his neighborhood's unofficial watchdog. She made it her business to report on the comings and goings of all her neighbors. She told Swanson she had seen two teenage girls drive off in his red Porsche about nine A.M. and that one of them was very pretty and wore nothing more than a dish towel for a skirt. It didn't take a clever attorney to figure out the identity of at least one of the girls.

"Aaron McAfee," Swanson said to the still assembled family after he got back from his call to Mrs. McGregor, "let me ask you something, and I want you to be honest with me since I do believe you when you say you cannot think of any reason why my car is missing."

"OK," Aaron said nervously.

"So, what if I connected a specific person to my missing car, and by specific, I mean Valerie Jean Smith? Can you think of any reason why your girlfriend, and I'd wager Mary Louise McAdams, would feel comfortable enough to park an easily identifiable car in front of our house, walk straight to the flowerpot where we keep our extra garage key, open the garage door, and drive off in my car as if doing so were the most natural thing in the world?"

"Gee, Dad, I . . ." Aaron began to say before Swanson stopped him with a look that he used to crush the spirit of even the most accomplished liar on the witness stand.

"Well, OK, I might have told Valerie that the car was mine and that she could borrow it if she wanted," Aaron stammered out, "but I wasn't serious. I mean I didn't think she'd take it so literally. I didn't even think she could drive a manual shift car or at least not well enough to drive off like that."

"Idiot," Aaron's sister said before her father glared at her with a judgelike look that said, "Enough!"

"I appreciate your honesty," Swanson said. "At least we know my car wasn't technically stolen so I'm not going to report it. But I will tell you this: if there is one scratch on that car you will pay to have it fixed. And as for your girlfriend, you will have the unpleasant task of telling her parents that you lied about the car and caused this mess. Do you understand me?"

"Yes, I do," Aaron said, a bit sheepishly like someone taken down on cross-examination.

"And may I say, for me personally, son," Swanson continued, "I completely agree with your sister: you *are* an idiot!"

The conversation between Aaron and his father took place a full four hours before Valerie Jean and Mary Louise pulled into the McAfee's driveway, opened the garage door, parked the car just where they had found it, and finally, as Carlton had suggested, wiped the car down with some old towels. Mary Louise dropped Valerie Jean off at her house and drove home in her mother's comfortable old boat to wait for her parents' call. It came right on cue after dinner. Unfortunately, Mary Louise didn't have the expected conversation.

"Didn't I tell you that Valerie Jean Smith would be nothing but trouble?" her mother said, with the exasperated tone of a parent at the end of their rope. "So, what exactly were you and Valerie Jean doing all day in Mr. McAfee's car?"

"Mom, how did you . . ." Mary Louise began, but that's as far as she got before her mother offered up eyewitness testimony from Mr. McAfee's neighbor and informed her that she and Valerie Jean were the talk of the town. She added that at least a dozen other mothers had called to see if they could do anything to ease the pain of having a criminal daughter; a few even offered to bring over a casserole.

"So, where did you go?" her mother asked, exasperated. "You were gone all day long. I'm afraid to ask!"

As there was no point in lying, Mary Louise told the truth.

"To the beach," she said.

"To the beach," her mother repeated. "My God in heaven. What were you thinking?"

The conversation went downhill from there. Mary Louise was completely unsuccessful in convincing her mother that she and Valerie Jean had had a perfectly innocent day together (leaving out the cocktails of course).

"That's all well and good," her mother said, "but you should know that the car you took is no more Aaron's than I am the queen of Sheba. It belongs to Mr. McAfee, and he's not happy in the least!"

"What?" Mary Louise stammered out, "It's not . . ."

"No, it's not," her mother said. "Who would give their teenager a car like that? Think about it, Mary Louise, think."

The next day everyone gathered in the McAfee's driveway for a group apology, Valerie Jean and Mary Louise were criticized for their irresponsibility and failure to employ even the barest bit of critical thinking from the start. Aaron was excoriated for his lies, especially for the source lie that he owned a Porsche 911 that he could let anyone borrow, including his girlfriend.

Once the parents talked it out among themselves and apologies were made and gratitude given and received, it was concluded no real harm had been done. There was even a tension-breaking chuckle here and there as Mary Louise and Valerie Jean described their day at the beach and how expertly Valerie had driven the car—a regular Mario Andretti, someone said.

Looking back on it, Valerie Jean was absolutely right, it was a better story than getting caught hijacking a family station wagon for an impromptu beach trip. And as for keeping the adventure a secret, getting caught did have an upside because it quickly became an envied story among all their friends.

Important life lessons were also learned that day, although not necessarily the ones they admitted to in the McAfee family's driveway.

The first lesson was to ask better questions. If something seems too good to be true, then it probably is.

The second lesson was an essential fact of life that Valerie Jean had apparently been born knowing. That is, it's OK to relax and live your life, because if you do, things always turn out fine in the end. Mostly.

7
Weston's Big Breakfast

ALTHOUGH HE KNEW IT WAS A BAD IDEA TO TRUST what a restaurant said about itself on a roadside billboard, Weston Smiley threw caution to the wind and pulled off I-40 to follow a blaze of road signs that eventually led him to Smiley's Café in downtown Granville, Tennessee.

Clearly, it was the restaurant's name that first caught his eye. How could it not? But what really caused him to abandon his first rule of interstate travel (if he can't see it from the road, it don't exist) was the picture of a plate of bacon and eggs with a side of cheese biscuits and grits positioned right under the restaurant's claim to fame: Best Breakfast in the State of Tennessee.

Although he knew the claim was overstated, Weston was primed for temptation because nothing resembling such comfort food had passed his lips in recent memory. At least not since his wife, Marjorie Jean, had watched a documentary about factory farming practices with their teenage daughter, Audrey May, who had become somewhat of a vegan evangelical since watching the film herself two years ago.

"Once you watch the film," Audrey May had told her mother in prepping her for the film, "you'll never put another bite of bile-filled chicken breast or hormone-laced beef in your mouth again!"

Although she was skeptical about her daughter's histrionics, Marjorie Jean agreed to watch the film on the condition that Audrey May wouldn't talk about veganism for at least a week or make groaning noises during family meals; even when chicken was on the menu.

Marjorie Jean watched the film a few days later, and as her daughter had predicted, she was absolutely disgusted, sickened really, by what she saw. Conveyor belts packed with screaming baby chicks zooming past hair-netted workers who plucked out the unacceptable ones like weeds yanked from an otherwise perfect lawn; vast warehouses full of chickens packed into shoebox-size containers, all forced to lay eggs until they died from exhaustion; cows tethered to high-tech milking machines relentlessly sucking their teats dry without mercy.

It was a hard film to watch, especially for Marjorie Jean who dearly loved all animals. She had once nursed an orphaned baby squirrel back to health, despite frequently calling all squirrels stupid tree rats, a malevolence usually triggered when one of them ate all the seeds from her bird feeder or hollowed out the last perfect, plump red tomato of the season seemingly minutes before she left the kitchen to pick it for the tomato sandwich she had been thinking about all morning.

But the straw that broke the camel's back, as Marjorie Jean liked to say, was the moment in the film when the camera trained its lens on the innocent eyes of a baby calf just seconds before a slaughterhouse worker shot a retracting stainless-steel rod through its brain with a pneumatic slaughter gun.

For Marjorie Jean, it was an image that sealed the deal and converted her in one heart-pounding moment as surely as the light of Jesus fills the empty souls of the newly saved and sets them on a better, more righteous path. No more Tuesday night meatloaf feasts, no more weekend steaks, and most piteously, not one serving more of her famous chicken pot pie casserole smothered in melted American cheese and topped with crushed RITZ crackers.

Initially Marjorie Jean's family thought this latest passion would fizzle out at some point since she had built a reputation over the years for hopping aboard one health or diet bandwagon or another, only to abandon it after a few months. So, when she announced the next day that the Smiley family was now officially vegan, no one panicked, reasoning—and not without evidence—that this too shall pass. Unfortunately, this time it did not.

A few years ago, Marjorie Jean had read an article about the health consequences of excessive salt consumption. At the time it had not occurred to her that something as basic as salt could be so lethal, so she declared a moratorium on the spot. It was a dietary detour for the Smiley family that ended when she served a Sunday dinner after church of tasteless roast beef, green beans, and boiled potatoes.

Weston, normally an agreeable person, was so outraged by such food waste sacrilege that he lashed out, declaring he now understood why perfectly good civilizations had vanished off the face of the earth for want of salt. The Smiley family, he said, was now at a similar crossroads.

Marjorie Jean rolled her eyes at Weston's dramatics but got up anyway and returned with a full saltshaker and banged it down authoritatively on the table in front of Weston. "It's sea salt," she said, "and I understand it's not nearly as deadly as normal table salt, but not by much."

Marjorie Jean's banishment of bread, based on a magazine article she had read, also ended in a dramatic fashion after Weston refused to eat his hamburger nestled between two limp lettuce leaves that unfortunately did nothing to prevent ketchup, mayonnaise, and mustard from squirting out with projectile accuracy onto his best shirts and pants no matter how carefully he wrapped the patty.

"Either we stop this nonsense," Weston had said at the time, making no effort to tamp down his frustration, "or from now on I am coming to the table shirtless, or maybe just in my skivvies to make it more convenient for you to hose me down in the backyard after dinner."

The image of Weston coming to her table nearly naked—as appealing as that might have been under the right circumstances—was enough to end Marjorie's breadless crusade, although as a compromise Weston agreed to eat only whole wheat bread, with all manner of seeds in it.

"The seeds and natural grains are good for you and your colon," Marjorie Jean told Weston with the confidence of an expert.

"Well, Marge, I can't disagree with you there," Weston offered in a tone that Marjorie Jean knew meant a punchline was soon to follow. "Just about every time I sit out on our deck a gob of bird shit finds me or my newspaper, and the one thing that I've noticed is that bird poop has lots of seeds in it. If that's any reliable measure of success."

After a month of Job-like patience waiting for Marjorie Jean's latest vegan dietary detour to find an exit ramp, everyone began to worry that Marjorie Jean's passion for the vegan lifestyle might not end—all except Audrey May, who was ecstatic beyond words. The fact is, once Marjorie Jean connected eating a chicken, pig, or cow to the sentient creatures she now knew animals to be, the thought of frying up even a "humanely" raised chicken breast made Marjorie Jean physically sick. As far as she was concerned, eating any animal or animal product was just as unthinkable as basting and roasting Flannery, the family's beloved corgi.

If there was any saving grace in all this, it was the fact that Marjorie Jean was a prize-winning cook, and so it wasn't much of a stretch for her to transition to vegan cooking, something she did as if her family's life depended on it, which she was convinced it did. She checked out every vegetarian and vegan book in the Greenwood Public Library, six in all. Then she ordered a dozen more books from the Fancy Kumquat, the town's new independent bookshop, which had opened up recently next to the old Greenwood Hardware and Supply Company.

Over the weeks that followed, she worked relentlessly, learning simple and complex ways to mimic the tastes, flavors, and textures of the foods her family loved. After a few months even Weston, a diehard meat eater, had lost his obsession for meat. As time went by, he even lost a few pounds and his cholesterol levels improved significantly, an outcome that surprised and delighted his internist.

"I don't know what Marjorie Jean is cooking for you these days," Weston's doctor said during his annual physical, "but tell her it's making her husband a much healthier man."

Weston grimaced. "Thanks, doc," he said, "but I don't think she needs any encouragement, if you don't mind."

One of the casualties of Marjorie Jean's vegan conversion that family members regretted most was the loss of their near-legendary

Thanksgiving feast, a meal family members recounted with a zeal usually reserved for religious conversion. When they heard of Marjorie Jean's new vegan lifestyle, the family was struck dumb with confusion and disbelief as they contemplated the upcoming meal Marjorie Jean was preparing. And they all wondered, and frankly feared, the same thing. How on earth could a turkey made of seitan or tofu (even if it was shaped like a turkey) be anything but awful? Not even to mention the near gagging thought of consuming vegan cheese biscuits, vegan macaroni and cheese (that just didn't seem possible), or—worst of all—vegan redeye gravy.

As it turned out, the meal Marjorie Jean served on Thanksgiving turned out to be a marvel of high-end cuisine, even if it was vegan. Uncle Bob, the family curmudgeon who always had something to complain about, gave the whole meal high praise, particularly the turkey loaf, which he said was the best turkey he'd eaten in years, even if it wasn't really turkey.

Audrey May was so enthusiastic she advised her mother to open a restaurant in downtown Greenwood, a move she said would go a long way toward converting the entire town to veganism. "There's an empty storefront right across the street from The Happy Clam, that fancy gift shop in town, so you're sure to have customers," Audrey May told her mother. Weston thought his daughter was being a bit optimistic as Greenwood was known far and wide for its annual barbeque festival, but he let it go.

His son, Hunter, was less enthusiastic, although when asked he did allow that the dinner was "pretty good." A qualified endorsement to be sure, but still remarkable because Bradley was an adolescent known for never offering even the slightest bit of hyperbolic praise about anything or anyone.

Smiley's Café was housed in a meticulously restored 1930s Woolworth storefront right in the middle of Granville. The restaurant was clearly the town's anchor business, at least based on a quick survey of the storefronts Weston made as he cruised down Main Street. One business did intrigue him enough to slow down for a closer look, a quirky variety store called The Disciple's Table apparently affiliated with a local church, given its tagline, Come In and Save with Jesus, which was painted on a four-by-six-foot piece of plyboard in neat red block letters on a white background that hung precariously over the shop's entrance.

Weston noted that the sign had been sloppily hung and had he lived in Granville, Weston would surely have offered to fix it as an unselfish act of community service, something he had a habit of offering based solely on his ability to offer it. It was a personality trait that had earned him the admirable moniker of "good ole boy," a distinction that followed him around like a respected professional acronym: Weston Lee Smiley, GOB. It was an honorific title, at least in Greenwood, outpacing by a considerable distance his harder-won advanced degree in organizational development.

The other positive sign of commercial vitality was a new gas station, called Red's Exxon, noteworthy for its professionally maintained landscaping, cheerful and inviting signage, and the power-washed sheen of cleanliness it exuded even from a distance. It was a modern-day oracle of consumerism that compelled travelers to pull off the road to buy coffee, soft drinks, sandwiches, extra-value-size bags of Cheetos and Chex Mix, six packs of Slim Jims, cheap sunglasses, and mildly offensive bumper stickers.

By the time Weston pushed open the heavy plate glass doors of Smiley's Café at 301 Main Street, Weston was so ravenously distracted by hunger he didn't notice Peter Simmons, the restaurant owner, or his catcher's mitt-size hand extended in his direction.

"Welcome," the amiable man said, grabbing Weston's unprepared hand and pumping it vigorously up and down as if he were working an old water pump. "I'm Peter Simmons, owner of Smiley's Café, and I'm glad you stopped by today. Would you like a table or booth this morning?"

"Booth, please," Weston said.

"Sure thing," Peter replied, gathering up a menu and a printed list of specials, and extending his arm toward the dining room. "I have a nice quiet booth right over here for you. Will others be joining you, or is it just you today?"

"No, just me."

"And is this your first time here?" Peter asked, as he walked Weston to the table.

"Yep, first time," Weston replied, "just passing through on my way to a client meeting in Nashville."

"And what's your business?" Peter asked in a genuinely interested tone of voice.

"I'm an organizational consultant," Weston answered.

"Might know a bit about that myself," Peter said, knowingly.

"Yep, I basically help companies and employees work together more efficiently," Weston said, "at least that's the idea."

"Well, good. Welcome to my company."

Peter stood by as Weston slid under the expansive tabletop that was in fact quiet with the added benefit of soft filtered light from a nearby floor-to-ceiling plate glass window that warmed his right shoulder like a comforting hand. Peter then handed Weston a menu and offered to bring a pot of coffee.

"I appreciate it, Peter," Weston said, before adding with a playful grin, "but I think it's only fair to warn you that there's a good chance I might order everything on the menu today."

"Thanks for letting me know. I'll alert the kitchen staff at once," Peter replied with a deadpan expression. Weston and Peter smiled at each other broadly, recognizing kindred jokesters.

Weston did not order everything on the menu that day at Smiley's, but he did an admirable job of eating nearly all the food that arrived at his table. As an appetizer, he ordered a full stack of pancakes topped with sausage. Then he ordered a Western omelet, a side of cheese grits, and extra bacon. Finally, for good measure—or to fully seal his coffin as Marjorie Jean would have said had she witnessed her husband's extraordinary vegan sacrilege—he ordered another side of bacon and country ham as a kind of refresher. He knew it was a ridiculous amount of food, but he was determined to binge while he had a chance: no jackfruit barbeque, no tofu bites, no vegan ham-and-cheese sandwiches.

By the time Peter came by Weston's table again, the remains of his meal had been cleared, except for the plate of bacon and country ham slices. Weston was leaning against the booth back and had turned slightly to allow one leg to partially stretch down the bench seat as if he were relaxing at home on his couch.

"So, did you enjoy your breakfast?" Peter asked.

"Did I ever," Weston said, dropping his leg off the seat. "Your highway sign is not lying. This *is* the best breakfast in the state of Tennessee."

"Glad to hear it," Peter said, "mind if I sit?"

"Please do," Weston said, gesturing toward the seat opposite him. Peter asked one of the passing servers to bring a fresh pot of coffee and two clean cups and then sat down.

"Well, I must admit, I'm impressed," Peter said, while pouring fresh coffee into the new mugs the server brought them. "You were dead serious about ordering everything on the menu."

"It's a bit embarrassing," Weston admitted as he pulled the steaming coffee cup his way. He picked up another piece of crisp bacon and took a hefty bite. "But I'm sort of like a man who's been stranded on an island with nothing to eat but coconuts," he continued, "except that on this island, instead of coconuts, what's hanging from the trees are packages of tofu."

"I understand," Peter said empathetically, "say no more. See it all the time. A devoted meat eater trapped in a family of recently converted vegans. And if it makes you feel any better you are not the first reluctant vegan or even vegetarian to fall off the wagon here."

"I'll bet," Weston said, "and you're right. I am not what you might call a fully engaged vegan, more like a conscript."

"So how did that happen?" Peter asked.

"Well, the answer to that is a bit of a saga," Weston said, "and I'm sure you have a lot to do other than listen to me whine about my wife's conversion to veganism."

"I do," Peter said, "but we've got a whole pot of coffee here, so let's hear it. I'd be interested in what would make a man eat that much food at one sitting."

Weston explained the circumstances and events leading up Marjorie Jean's conversion to veganism: how she had watched the vegan propaganda film, about his wife's history of going off on one health improvement tear or another, and how the family hoped Marjorie Jean would come around as she had always done before and drop her vegan obsession. Peter listened intently and without judgment, offering up "I'm listening" verbal cues like a therapist.

"Don't get me wrong, she's a wonder and a force of nature in the kitchen," Weston told Peter, "an extraordinary cook, really. She made a mushroom steak last week that I could have sworn was sirloin. I don't know how she does it."

"Still," he continued, "there is just something about real pork, bacon, sausage, steak, eggs, butter, and cheese. There's just no replacement for that."

"I hear you, my friend," Peter said. "Maybe I should hire your wife to cook for me. I have been thinking about expanding our menu to offer vegan options."

"Heaven, help us, "Weston said, "Marjorie Jean doesn't need encouragement. Our daughter, Audrey May, has been after her mother for months to open a vegan restaurant in Greenwood. And to make matters worse, our son, Hunter, now says he's thinking about going vegan. Good God!"

"That's rough, my friend," Peter said emphatically.

"So, what's your story, Peter?" Weston asked, thinking the restaurant owner had heard enough about his vegan family. "How'd you end up with a restaurant in Granville, Tennessee? Are you a local?"

"No," Peter said, smiling, "and what I'm doing here is somewhat of a shaggy dog story as well."

"Well, I've got time if you do," Weston said, picking up the coffee carafe to test the weight. "There's even some coffee left."

As it turned out, Peter Simmons, aka Smiley, was a former insurance executive from Chicago with a lifelong passion for cooking. He had gone to The Culinary Institute of America in Poughkeepsie for a while but gave up that dream when he fully considered how difficult it was to make any money in the restaurant business, so he moved to his plan B, which was getting an MBA from the University of Chicago.

The degree helped him build a financially rewarding career at McKinsey & Company. He was a natural-born leader who knew how to navigate the cutthroat world of upper management politics and resolve conflict without getting in the middle of the fight. Still, the idea of running a restaurant never left him. He had, however, put his chef training to good use throughout his life, impressing girlfriends, including his wife who said she married Peter because he could cook. He always mesmerized his dinner guests by serving meals so beautifully plated that they often hesitated a few minutes before eating their meal as if they were being forced to dismantle a meticulously built sculpture for the scrap metal.

Such moments of joy had been satisfying enough for Peter until five years ago when he had a flat tire just shy of the I-40 exit for Granville. "Call it luck, the random universe, or fate, but that flat tire changed my life," Peter told Weston as he spun the tale of moving to Granville and opening his restaurant.

"It all started with a conversation I had with Red Smith," Peter recounted, "who was the fella who came to tow my car off the highway."

"Hey, wait a minute," Weston interjected, "is this the same Red who owns Red's Exxon down the street?"

"The same," Peter confirmed.

"Anyway," Peter continued, "while we were riding back to the station in his tow truck, he mentioned that a familiar Japanese car company was building a factory right outside of town. He told me I should invest while the price of real estate was low."

"Naturally, I took this information with a grain of salt as it's generally not a good idea to act on investment tips given out by random tow truck drivers. Still, for some reason I checked out what Red told me, and it turned out he was telling the truth. A Honda plant was being built just a few miles outside of town, and the real estate here was dirt cheap, so I bit."

Peter recalled how he had taken a cruise down Main Street after Red fixed his tire. He said something had clicked when he saw the Woolworth building and, in that moment, a fully developed vision of his life as a restaurant owner entered his mind. When he got home, he told his wife about his epiphany. He flew back to Nashville a few weeks later and bought the building. Then he told his CEO he would be leaving the company in a year's time.

"Everyone thought I was nuts," Peter said, "including our children and maybe even Evelyn, my wife, who couldn't imagine leaving Chicago. But after a few trips to Nashville, she came around. She loves it here and can't imagine living in Chicago again, especially during the winter."

"The thing is," Peter said, "the cosmos is always talking to you, even if the messenger is a guy named Red who happens to be driving a tow truck. The trick is to listen to what the universe is saying, then all you have to do is muster the courage to make it happen. You know, roll the dice and expect the best."

Peter laughed at his own homespun wisdom. The sound of his cackle echoed off the restaurant's newly painted pressed tin ceiling before settling like a comfortable blanket on the restored lunch counter and generous leatherette dining booths.

"And here's something else I've learned," Peter said as he got up to leave. "You never know where an ordinary conversation will take you."

※

It was a simple conversation in a slow-moving grocery store checkout line twenty-five years earlier that led to Weston's first date with Marjorie Jean. He had stopped by the grocery store to buy cereal, milk, RITZ crackers, cheddar cheese, and frozen pizzas, a fifteen-minute stop that pretty much completed Weston's entire grocery list for the week.

As it turned out, Marjorie Jean, who was ahead of him in line pushing a shopping cart so full of groceries that Weston could not help but stare in awe at both the cart's abundance and the beauty of the woman pushing it. When Marjorie Jean noticed Weston ogling her cart—or her, she wasn't sure which one—she spoke up, not to embarrass him for his interest, but because that's just what Marjorie did, talk to anyone and everyone.

"I know, it looks like I'm cooking for an entire army," Marjorie Jean said as if they'd known each other for years, "but the truth is I offered to cook dinner for my family, including aunts, uncles, cousins, children, and apparently anyone else who wants to come." She laughed, then said with mock indignation, "I mean, normally if you offer to do something that's clearly too much, people object in some way. They'll say, 'Oh, no, you don't have to do that,' or 'Let me help,' or at least, 'What can I bring?' But in this case, nothing. Nada. Not a word. Just a lot of 'It is so awfully nice of you to offer.' So, I'm on the hook for the entire feast. It's a good thing I like to cook!"

Marjorie laughed at her own joke, and Weston was immediately captivated by her humor and good nature. "So, what kind of party are you having?" Marjorie asked Weston, looking down at his near empty shopping cart.

"I'm not having a party," he told her. "I'm just having some friends over to watch a football game." This was patently untrue because Weston hated watching any kind of sports on television. The truth was, he was embarrassed to admit he ate so poorly compared to Marjorie Jean.

On their first date a few weeks later, Weston admitted he never watched football and that cooking was like the dark arts to him. When Weston tells the story of how he met Marjorie Jean, he often says that the only reason she married him was to improve his diet. It was a joke that still got a chuckle because there was some truth to it. Boiling water was still a significant culinary challenge for him.

As for Marjorie Jean's truth, she did have an affinity for saving, improving, and fixing things: mending torn shirts, sewing missing buttons on pants, repairing abandoned chairs and tables, and improving the diet of goodhearted, slightly lost people. And, lately, saving every animal on the face of the planet.

※

Peter stopped by to say goodbye as Weston gathered up his belongings. "Hi, my friend," Peter said, sitting down again across from Weston. "I'm glad you stopped by today. Here's my card just in case your wife wants to get into the restaurant business. Sounds like she's a serious vegan chef."

Weston laughed as he took the card. "I'll mention it to her when I tell her about the breakfast of grapefruit and tofu scramble you served me this morning."

Peter laughed.

"Yep, I suspect you're not ready to be married to a working vegan chef, but I'm not kidding about offering more vegan options," Peter said, with a business tone of voice. "Nashville is a more sophisticated food destination than people think. There are lots of first-rate restaurants there, including some new vegan restaurants that are quite good. Got to keep up with my competition, you know."

"Oh, I understand," Weston said. "And if Marjorie Jean keeps up her enthusiasm for being vegan, who knows, the next time I stop by for breakfast I could be a fully committed vegan rather than a conscript. Hell, I might be asking for your new vegan menu and thanking you for saving the world."

"You think?" Peter replied, smiling.

"Maybe," Weston said. "I'm not one to rule anything out. And if I do come by again, and especially if I happen to be with Marjorie Jean who sometimes comes along with me when I see my client here, I'm giving you permission ahead of time to intervene and ask your chef to put real bacon bits in my tofu scramble. Is that a deal?"

Peter laughed. "That's a deal," he said.

"And by the way," Peter continued, holding up a Smiley's carry-out container, "here's a bacon, lettuce, and tomato sandwich on white bread for the road. Just in case you get hungry on the way down to Nashville."

"Unlikely, but thank you," Weston said, accepting the takeout bag, "but you never know. It is forty miles and a lot can happen in that distance."

"Yes, I know," Peter said, "I surely do know that's true."

Weston turned and walked out of the restaurant, and by the time he got to his car he was already thinking about a good spot to stop and eat his BLT on his way down to Nashville.

8

A Game of Chess

ROBERT LEE JOHNSON NEVER CARED MUCH FOR games, something he traced to growing up on a small farm just outside of town where daily chores left little time for such idle distractions and a father who often reminded him of his own joyless conviction about games.

"Games are for the leisure class," his father always declared at the mention of games, "and son, that ain't us." And so, outside a few rounds of Monopoly with his own children and the occasional card game with his two best friends, Carter Dean Jackson and Swanson McAfee, who he met most Wednesday mornings at Dixie's Diner, Robert Lee managed to avoid playing games all together.

Then one morning Carter Dean showed up with a chessboard and set it up in the middle of the group's regular faded Formica table, the one by the window with a panoramic view of Green Street. It was a change in setting Robert Lee didn't immediately notice as he approached the table with a newspaper in one hand and a steaming cup of coffee in the other that diner owner Dixie Leigh McBride had pushed in his direction as they exchanged morning pleasantries.

When he did notice the chessboard, Robert Lee felt immediately anxious, as if he'd been caught committing a social faux pas, like forgetting to hold a door open for an elderly woman or perhaps stopping his car in the middle of a pedestrian crosswalk so that everyone had to walk around him. He immediately began concocting face-saving ways to beg off from their meeting.

Swanson, who was already sitting at their table, had an altogether different reaction as he passively watched Carter Dean set up the chessboard. He was delighted because chess offered considerable potential for sparring with his lifelong friend.

"Didn't know you owned a chessboard, Carter Dean," Swanson said, with a tone of mock surprise in his voice.

"Yep," Carter Dean replied, "as a matter of fact I do."

"Excellent," Swanson replied, his lips poised over the rim of an oversize mug that Dixie kept under her counter for regulars like Swanson and the rest of the coffee club. "And I have to say I'm pleased you've taken the initiative to raise the level of discourse at this table. However, are you sure you know how to play? It's quite a sophisticated game. Would you like some pointers on how to play?" Carter Dean smiled, unperturbed by his friend's familiar taunts.

"Oh, I know how to play just fine," Carter Dean said, picking up a black king from his side of the board and pointing it directly at Swanson like a weapon. "And as much as I appreciate your offer, counselor," he said, "I'd say the real question here is whether you can back up your BS by risking a few Ben Franklins on a game."

Swanson smiled, then leaned into his Atticus Finch persona, the one he'd used for the last twenty years to win over dozens of juries from Georgia to Washington, DC. "First," he said, "the strength of my finances is well-known to this community, but perhaps the real question here is one of professional ethics. That is, is it ethical for a clearly superior player to take advantage of a less capable one? This is especially true," he continued, "when one of the wagering parties has a long history of overestimating their talents and capabilities."

Robert Lee arrived at the coffee club's table in the middle of this escalating insult contest but said nothing because experience had taught him that once Carter Dean and Swanson locked horns it was best to observe from a safe distance, like watching a fistfight in the street, close enough to see, but not so close you can't run away if things get out of hand.

"I appreciate your concern," Carter Dean said, "but I'll be fine. And by the way, I will only accept cash for your losses. I don't care a thing about owning your new, stupidly fancy sports car, if you still own it, that is, or perhaps the repo man has already paid a visit to your garage?"

"No, it's still in my garage, and yes, I do, in fact, own it outright without lien or any other encumbrances or claims on its ownership."

"Happy to hear it, my friend," Carter Dean said, smiling. "It must feel good to finally be out of debt." Both men chuckled, happy to call their mock war of wills a draw for now.

While waiting for Swanson and Carter Dean to finish their predictable insult contest, Robert Lee slid into his place beside Carter Dean and began perusing the latest edition of the *Greenwood Clarion*. The paper, published daily, focused mainly on local and regional news, although it always had a comprehensive summary of state, national, and international developments and how these machinations of politics and commerce outside the borders of Greenwood might affect the town's economy and well-being. There was, of course, comprehensive coverage of city council meetings, high school and community college graduation ceremonies, and perhaps most important, a significant sports section devoted to local and regional teams including the beloved Greenwood High School football team, the Hornets. Editorially, the paper veered toward conservative and generally steered clear of anything salacious or controversial.

Still, a few years ago, the *Clarion* had devoted a great deal of space to the story of Stewart Peabody, a local resident who had discovered a large cache of double eagle gold coins in his backyard while digging a fishpond for his wife. Initially, the paper covered the discovery as a feel-good, human-interest story, at least until the provenance of the coins created a divisive controversy about Stewart's right to keep the coins.

One camp of the citizenry had supported the immutable law of "finders keepers, losers weepers." The other camp believed the courts should decide the matter. Opinion largely tilted toward the finders-keepers side. In the end, the courts devised a solution that pleased nearly everyone in town, and both camps had been forced to find something else to be outraged about.

One particularly salacious controversy that clearly did not find its way into the *Clarion* was an illegally distributed video of the paper's well regarded publisher, Larry Fine, who was filmed engaged in carnal relations with a woman (not his wife) by a pool at a high-end Virginia Beach hotel. Both of these local controversies neither disappointed nor outraged the coffee club members because they had long ago stopped being surprised by anyone's ability to make a mess of their lives.

"So, is there anything we should know about?" Carter Dean asked, gesturing toward Robert Lee's open newspaper.

"No, not much," he replied, "no disasters, controversies, or embarrassing revelations, same old, which is good for someone in the insurance business, I always say."

"Glad to hear it," Carter Dean said.

"So, do you play chess, RL?" Carter Dean asked. RL was Robert Lee's nickname.

"Not really," Robert Lee answered. "I'm not much for games. Hell, I can't win at Go Fish with my own kids, even when I try."

"I find that hard to believe," Carter Dean said, "and even if it's true, I think you can always teach an old dog a new trick."

"Maybe," Robert Lee said, "but that largely depends on the dog."

It was an unconfident response that was foreign to both Carter Dean and Swanson, two men who had succeeded in fabulous and profitable ways, despite growing up on the bottom rung of the social ladder in Greenwood's west end. Carter Dean was now one of the state's most successful real estate developers, and Swanson was a flamboyant and sought-after trial lawyer.

Their success had brought them money and status and eventually invitations to join the region's most prestigious country and social clubs, including the Tarheel Social Club, a place known for its smartly dressed servers who poured coffee from gleaming silver carafes into bone china cups and wiped away dribbles with stiff, pressed, white, linen napkins.

Although they enjoyed these well-earned privileges, neither Carter Dean nor Swanson took regular advantage of them that often, preferring Dixie's coffee served to them in their own stained, chipped mugs with a neatly folded, and mostly useless, paper napkin tucked underneath the cup to catch the always copious dribbles.

The truth was, despite their successful careers, both men felt a little uncomfortable and sometimes even a bit irritated by the assumptions that their other country club or social club members made about one another. Not everyone came from a well-to-do family or had paintings of celebrated ancestors hanging over their generous ancestral fireplaces. Such assumptions of sharing the same White privilege sometimes annoyed them so much they sought refuge in the Tarheel Social Club's mahogany-paneled bar or out on the patio of their country club with its meticulously manicured gardens surrounded with an endless expanse of freshly cut bright green fairways. It was somewhat of a tradition for one of them to trot out their favorite inside joke at these times.

"I guess you and I were not to the manner born," Swanson might say in his sophisticated Southern drawl. Then they'd both chuckle as if they'd just heard the joke for the first time. It was left unaddressed whether or not the wellspring of this humor was the irony of it or simply the uncomfortable sting of their own hypocrisy. Be that as it may, they enjoyed the joke and always told it without malice or envy or self-satisfaction.

Swanson and Carter Dean made their first moves while Robert Lee was getting a coffee refill. Although Swanson had an advantage—he'd played for Princeton University's chess team—both were accomplished chess players. In fact, Swanson still relied on the game's strategic-thinking disciplines to anticipate his courtroom opponent's next move, a frustrating tactic that brought both admiration and ire from those he argued against.

Swanson McAfee taught himself chess by reading books and initially playing against himself. It was his algebra teacher who became his chess partner in the ninth grade who was also the first to recognize Swanson's extraordinary intellect and encouraged him to aim for goals beyond a high school degree and steady work in his family subsistence scrap metal hauling business. He had taken his teacher's challenge that he could do better with astonishing results.

Carter Dean's chess credentials were less impressive, but still formidable. He had played his first game with an intern at Greenwood Hospital many years ago while recuperating from surgery to repair a torn ligament in his knee, the result of a high school football injury. At the University of Georgia, where his high school football skills got him a full-ride finance and business degree, he found many worthy opponents, including members of the university's chess club who were flabbergasted to be beaten by the school's star quarterback.

After graduation Carter Dean took a job at Greenwood Community Bank. Within a few years he'd saved enough money to buy his first investment property, a small one-story rambler on the border of the city's most exclusive eastside neighborhood. He had renovated the house on weekends and then sold it for a handsome profit, an experience that firmly set the entrepreneur hook.

More than twenty years later, the Carter Dean Group developed and sold properties throughout the region and employed twenty-four people full-time. Around town, dozens of billboards and bus stop rain shelters featured Carter Dean's still youthful, square-jawed face, and as a consequence he was a true small-pond celebrity. Strangers often stopped by the coffee club booth to ask if Carter Dean was the same person they'd seen on the billboards.

"The same," Carter Dean always replied, offering a familiar joke about the camera's magic and how it made him look twenty years younger. People liked Carter Dean's easy-going, self-deprecating manner, and so most supplicants walked away with both a positive impression and one of his business cards.

Robert Lee's personal history, at least until recently, was less storied or interesting. After graduating from college with a business degree, he took the first job offered to him by a major insurance company. He thrived in the structured, predictable corporate environment for nearly a dozen years and had been on his way to becoming executive vice president when he decided, seemingly out of the blue, to start his own company, the RL Johnson Insurance Agency, in downtown Greenwood. His business success astounded him, and over the years he had become a trusted community leader known for his favorite business expression, "Slow and steady wins the day." It was the perfect tagline for an insurance agent, although he often wondered if such a philosophy limited the amount of serendipity he could expect in life.

When Robert Lee thought about the group's disparate personalities, it puzzled him why their friendship had endured all these years. He didn't have a good answer. Swanson was charismatic and exceptionally smart, Carter Dean was competitive and friendly to everyone, and RL was neither competitive nor exceptionally outgoing. In fact, he was most comfortable behind his desk immersed in what others would consider tedious administrative work, such as studying the details of a new insurance offering.

When Robert Lee returned to the table with his coffee, neither contestant acknowledged him. Swanson and Carter Dean stared at the chessboard like two lions on the African savannah considering the same wildebeest for lunch. Then suddenly, with a deliberate and confident motion, Carter Dean reached out and advanced his knight. He smiled broadly as he released his grip. Swanson's expression didn't change as he relaxed back into his booth seat and reached for his coffee.

"Hum, knight to C six. You sure you want to make that move?" Swanson asked, sipping his coffee. "You can change your mind if you want. I'll let you."

"Damn it, Swanson," Carter Dean said, "just play the game. I don't have all day for your bullshit."

"OK," Swanson replied, "just let it be noted that I gave you a chance." He leaned forward to pinch a white bishop between his thumb and index finger. "Bishop to C three," he said, slowly moving his hand away. He smiled like he had just revealed new evidence to an opponent in court.

Nothing about this game made any sense to Robert Lee. Although he had read about how all expert players possessed an encyclopedic recall of winning strategies, he couldn't imagine having the raw intelligence or confidence to use these strategies against an opponent. Just the thought of holding dozens of confrontational moves in his head made him dizzy with anxiety.

It was not that Robert Lee had never known the thrill of competition or what it felt like to win a prize. In college he had toyed with the idea of majoring in journalism and signed up as a reporter for his college newspaper, "just to test the waters," he told himself. By sheer accident he had stumbled across a story of corruption and payback involving the state's most powerful senator, revealed to him by a disgruntled former intern he'd met at a beer keg party. A more experienced staff member joined him to report the story, an impressive investigative piece that embarrassed the party in power (especially after the story was picked up by the *Washington Post*) and precipitated the loss of several key congressional seats in the next election cycle. He and his co-reporter won a statewide student journalism award.

8 – A Game of Chess

Although the notoriety did raise his collegiate profile, especially among his progressive female classmates, he ultimately decided against switching majors to journalism once he learned that even the best reporters were paid abysmal salaries. Notoriety is fine, he thought, and positively affecting the world even better, but that's no substitute for a steady, well-paid job. He stuck with his business degree.

It was a decision he had never regretted. He'd married a hometown girl, Jeanie Fay Smith, and within a few years they'd built a house in the nicest part of town and soon outfitted it with two well-behaved and predictable children, Eileen and Robert Lee Jr., both of whom loved their father dearly. All had been fine until a few years ago when Robert Lee began having restless feelings as if he'd forgotten to do something. He couldn't explain the persistent anxiety, nor could he say what he was anxious about or what he was being called to do, as Pastor James might have framed Robert Lee's feelings.

Oddly enough, the answer came to him while waiting to get a haircut at Penzy's Barbershop on Green Street. He was flipping through a months-old, dog-eared magazine when he ran across an article about a highly paid movie studio executive who had quit her job to hike the Pacific Coast Trail. It was, according to the article, a decision that had transformed the executive's life. The fact that Robert Lee even read the article was unusual because he was not known for his love of the outdoors, despite his farming background.

In fact, his dislike of the wilderness was a recurring family joke based on the few backpacking trips he and Jeanie Fay had taken in the Blue Ridge Mountains before they married. He had complained bitterly about the dirt in the tent and sleeping on a backpacking pad, which he claimed was the thickness of a detailed insurance policy. Still, reading about the woman's experience stirred something in him.

By the time he was sitting in Mario Penzy's barber chair, he had formulated a plan; he too would go on an epic hike, but instead of the Pacific Coast Trail he would hike the East Coast equivalent, the Appalachian Trail.

Immaculately groomed and shaven, he had returned home and told Jeanie Fay what he was considering. At first Jeanie Fay thought he was joking, reminding him that it was her recollection that he didn't much like backpacking or car camping for that matter, even when he was twenty years younger.

"My memory of you and camping is that you spent a lot of time complaining about the dirt, and having to sleep on the ground," his wife reminded him. "And even when I took all my clothes off in the tent, you kept yours on because you thought the tent was filled with mosquitos. If you ask me, I'd call that a missed opportunity." She smiled, inviting him to chuckle along with her, which he did.

Despite his wife's initial lukewarm reception, Robert Lee began researching his proposed hike. He found a comprehensive AT guide (as trail enthusiasts called it) at the Greenwood Public Library. It offered advice on every aspect of hiking the AT: what equipment to take, how to pack, what to wear, what and how to cook, trail etiquette, where to find the best vistas, and what a hiker should and shouldn't worry about.

Jeanie Fay decided not to openly discourage her husband, thinking that once he fully considered the realities of a months-long backpacking trek—the bugs, dirt, rain, and not to mention the physical stamina required—he'd change his mind or maybe hike for a week, call it a day, and phone her to suggest they meet at a bed-and-breakfast for a romantic getaway. But when one of their spare bedrooms began to fill up with backpacking equipment—bought on weekend trips to a sporting goods store in Raleigh—she decided her only option was to support him, even if it made no sense to her.

"Well, Robert Lee," she said one day, "I can see you're serious about having this adventure, and if it's something you really want to do, then I'm here to support you, even if it seems like an odd thing for a fifty-eight-year-old insurance executive to do." With that she handed him an oblong package. "This should help you get some sleep," she said, "something I suspect hikers need."

What Robert Lee found when he opened the package was a bedroll the size of a bread loaf that inflated to a sleeping pad four inches thick. Robert Lee was so happy and filled with love that he nearly cried, a memorable emotional watermark in itself.

A few weeks later he called his insurance agency staff together to formally announce his forthcoming sabbatical. Everyone was mystified as to why a normally even-tempered boss would suddenly decide to spend months hiking in the woods. Still, the announcement did solve a mystery that had consumed the staff for weeks: why had RL been wearing hiking boots instead of his signature shiny leather loafers and colorful socks. Most just assumed Robert Lee was having trouble with his feet. No one dared mention the wardrobe change for fear of being rude.

"I guess you all know my motto is slow and steady," he told his gathered staff of a dozen employees, "and as you all can attest, it's advice I've always followed. But today I'm announcing something wholly unexpected and perhaps even surprising."

With that teaser, he had revealed his plans. Most of the employees chuckled because it seemed such a ridiculous notion. He had chuckled with them at first but quickly let them know he was serious. Every face in the room suddenly registered profound puzzlement, not unlike someone who's just seen a naked hitchhiker standing on the side of the road. Robert Lee waited a few beats for his employees to confirm with one another what they'd heard. Then he told them that Melvin Lanford, the company's vice president, would be in charge while he was away.

"And no," he said, reacting to his staff's still baffled faces, "I have not lost my mind. I will return. No need to worry about that."

Of course, Robert Lee's announcement did not end speculation about his decision to go on a hiking sabbatical; it just opened the floodgates for speculation as to the "real reason" he was leaving town.

Predictably, a good percentage of the speculation involved another woman, a farfetched notion as it was widely known that he and Jeanie Fay were happily married. Some ventured that Robert Lee was having a midlife crisis, or he just wanted to find himself. Those of this opinion, with similar comedic timing, said that if Robert Lee really needed to find himself, then they'd advise him to go find the nearest mirror instead of taking a difficult hike. Some less charitable speculation also emerged, including the ludicrous notion that Robert Lee would soon announce he was gay or was caught up in some nefarious criminal activity. These ideas got no traction whatsoever.

The day before informing his employees, Robert Lee had told his family about his plans while they sat around the dinner table eating healthy slices of Jeanie Fay's signature pecan pie. All were generally supportive except Eileen, his daughter, who was highly skeptical.

"Family, I have some news to share," he announced in a businesslike tone more appropriate for sharing staff reductions.

"I will be taking some time off from my business this coming summer." He immediately realized that leaving out the words "good news" at the beginning was a mistake because tears welled up in Eileen's eyes and even Robert Lee Jr. looked crestfallen.

"Sorry, nothing is wrong. I'm fine and my business is fine. And no, your mother and I are not getting a divorce," he said chuckling. "Nothing like that. It's good news. At least I think so."

"So, the news is," he continued, "I plan to hike the Appalachian Trail—at least a good portion of it—this coming summer." He had to wait for Eileen and Robert Lee Jr.'s initial hysterical laughter to die down, so he could repeat himself, adding emphatically, "It's not a joke. I'm really going to do this." The mood of the gathering dramatically changed, and Eileen struggled to prevent a vulgar expletive from leaving her mouth.

"Backpacking? For God's sake, Dad," Eileen nearly screamed "you're barely even a car camper. Have you forgotten how much you hate sleeping on the ground? Or that you don't like getting dirty or being bit by mosquitos? You've got to be kidding."

Robert Lee Jr. was more supportive because he had hiked significant portions of the Appalachian Trail one summer with his girlfriend.

"That's great, Dad," he said empathetically, "but I'd feel better if you didn't go alone. I can tell you from experience that the hike is pretty demanding. I just worry about you. What if you sprain your ankle or fall into a ravine? It's not a walk in the park."

"I appreciate your concern, Robert Lee," he reassured his son, "but you know me. If anyone should be able to assess risk, it's me. Don't forget I'm an insurance guy. It's what I do." He smiled, inviting his son to follow suit.

"No, Dad, I didn't forget you're an insurance guy," Robert Lee Jr. had said with a pained smile, "in fact, that's just what worries me."

As it turned out, Robert Lee's slow and steady personality allowed him to train for the hike like a newly enthused marathon runner. He began taking frequent short solo backpacking excursions to test his equipment and the accuracy of what he'd been reading about hiking. One thing he had to admit at the end of the first few hiking trips was that bears clearly had an advantage when it came to shitting in the woods.

After a few months of these weekend trips, he stopped wearing suits to work and began wearing hiking pants and shirts with a breathable flap across the shoulder, mostly tan or olive green in color. In truth, everyone thought his new look was less ridiculous than his previous fashion choice of wearing expensive gray suits and muddy hiking boots on his feet.

Robert Lee ultimately completed a good portion of the AT without major incident. His business and marriage survived, and respect among his family, friends, and employees increased exponentially—especially among his friends Carter Dean and Swanson. He frequently wrote letters to them, which they read out loud on Wednesday mornings as if their friend were on a walkabout in Australia or on an expedition in the darkest heart of Africa.

Robert Lee's eloquence as a writer also impressed Carter Dean and Swanson, a narrative talent they agreed was connected to his days as a student journalist. Robert Lee often went on for pages describing the beauty and majesty of the landscape, naming flora, fauna, and wildlife like a naturalist. He provided detailed descriptions of the people he met, offering up interesting vignettes about their lives and what had drawn them to hike the AT. He wrote powerfully of the hardships he overcame and how good it felt to emerge on the other side, recounting with a philosopher's existential insight about how he intended to live the rest of his life.

"You know," Carter Dean said to Swanson after reading a particularly long letter he'd received the previous weekend, "I must admit Robert Lee has surprised me. I would have never thought him capable of veering so completely off the well-beaten path. He's a different person."

"I agree," Swanson said, putting his mug down on the group's table with a heavy thud. "I always considered him a damn good insurance agent, but the mettle he's shown on this journey has astounded me. Hell, I'm even a little proud of our boy."

Carter Dean nodded and raised his coffee cup in Swanson's direction. "Here's to you, RL. You've made the coffee club proud."

"Hear, hear," they said in unison.

Robert Lee's sabbatical did in fact precipitate positive changes in his life. When he returned, he was more optimistic, confident, and adventurous, but one aspect of his personality remained immutable, his distaste for games. Sure, he had played cards with his trail mates to pass the time—a few rounds of Crazy Eights or Hearts and even a bit of poker using pebbles as chips—but these fond experiences did nothing to improve his general attitude toward or interest in games. That's why Carter Dean's chessboard on their table, even six months after completing his life-changing AT hike, still provoked extreme anxiety.

"It's your turn, Robert Lee," Carter Dean said, looking at Robert Lee after Swanson's impressive checkmate victory over him. "Maybe you can teach the counselor some humility."

"I doubt it," RL replied. "I don't really know how to play chess, and judging from the way you two play, it doesn't look like it's something I can learn to do on the fly."

"You may have a point, RL, but don't worry," Carter Dean said, holding up a cloth bag and shaking the contents to make it rattle like a maraca. "I just happen to have a set of checkers, and I know you can play that."

"That I cannot deny," Robert Lee replied, trying not to sound disappointed. "I do know how to play that game."

Carter Dean replaced the chess pieces with black and red plastic checker pieces and slid the board between Robert Lee and Swanson. Then he sat back in the booth. "OK, RL," he said, "you're up, and don't worry, Swanson's not near as smart as he thinks he is."

"Smart enough to take you down with relative ease, I wager," Swanson said, smiling at his friend.

"I'd suggest you focus on your new opponent," he replied. "And don't forget that Robert Lee found enlightenment on his pilgrimage, and he might have brought back some of that secret mojo he wrote to us about and use it to put you in your place."

"Bring it on," Swanson remarked, with a bit of unintended swagger.

Who can say whether it was his trail mojo, but Robert Lee beat Swanson in two out of three games, the two extra games insisted on by Swanson after he lost the first game. Carter Dean, of course, teased his friend mercilessly and praised Robert Lee as if he were a chess grand champion.

"You played him like a violin," he told Robert Lee. "He never had a chance." Swanson didn't react to Carter Dean's taunts and merely smiled as he reset the checker pieces.

"I would like a chance to redeem myself," Swanson said. "How about the best of two out of three?" Robert Lee surprised himself and agreed to Swanson's challenge with a bit of his own Swanson-inspired swagger.

"That's fine, Swanson," Robert Lee said. "I would never want to be known as someone who lacked grace in victory."

Swanson won the second game, but RL took the deciding round, a solid victory that Swanson was forced to acknowledge the clear win.

"That was impressive," Swanson admitted. "I was beaten fair and square. Congratulations."

Before his hike, Robert Lee might have deflected the compliment and said he was just lucky, a comment that quickly destroyed any pretense of power or competence and minimized the positive feelings he'd just earned. His reaction this time was different.

"Thanks, Swanson," he said. "I appreciate that. I guess it just goes to show maybe you *can* teach an old dog new tricks."

"Now you got it," Swanson said, standing up to get one final refill before heading to his office. "I'm proud of you," he said, "and that's something you've earned the right to own."

Robert Lee smiled uncomfortably and turned his head to stare out the window. Just then a bus passed with a placard on it advertising the Carter Dean Group. He watched the bus disappear down the street and imagined what it would feel like to have an advertisement for the RL Johnson Insurance Agency on the side of a bus with his picture smiling down at pedestrians and motorists. The idea still embarrassed him, but not nearly as much as it used to.

9

Henry Lee's Bird

VISITING THE GREENWOOD HUMANE SOCIETY WAS the last thing on Henry Lee Daniel's mind when he left his house that morning to pick up bread and milk from the mini-mart.

Yet, there he was, standing in his kitchen with a bright-eyed parrot on his shoulder that seemed eager to mesmerize his audience by showing off his fire-engine red breast feathers, sunflower-colored wings, and orange tail feathers streaked with dashes of vibrant blue as he strutted back and forth like a runway model.

Unfortunately, Mary Anne, Henry Lee's wife, was not in the least bit mesmerized by the bird's presence in her pristine kitchen. In fact, had she not been so deathly afraid of birds and all the nasty parasites and pathogens she believed they carried, she would have snatched the surprised bird off Henry Lee's shoulder and thrown it out the back door like a dustpan full of crumbs she'd just swept off the kitchen floor.

The fact is, Mary Anne initially hated Henry Lee's parrot and not just because she thought birds were best enjoyed from a distance of at least fifty yards. No, what really worried Mary Anne about having a bird inside her house was what she said was their "nasty" habit of relieving themselves "willy-nilly" whenever they felt like it, a thought that nearly sent her into convulsions of disgust.

It was these two concerns, mites and bird shit, that dominated their first arguments about Henry Lee's pet bird, even though she knew full well her fears were baseless and irrational. Still, it was the best argument she had at the time, so she felt obliged to trot out these fears to prop up her case against the parrot.

"Well, they don't call it bird flu for nothing," she said almost sheepishly as a way to cap off her argument, a statement that caused Henry Lee to shake his head in frustration.

"First of all, Mary Anne," Henry Lee responded, "birds are actually very clean animals, and as far as their personal habits go, I was told this one was house-trained."

Henry Lee didn't really buy the house-trained claim offered by the Humane Society volunteer who convinced him to adopt the parrot, but he used it as ammunition anyway. He later watched a YouTube video and learned that parrots, unlike dogs, don't understand the idea of treats so they are essentially untrainable. The online expert did offer a few "strategies" that might reduce paper towel use, but he ultimately admitted the best anyone could hope for, as far as bird household etiquette training goes, was somewhere between "pretty good" and "somewhat successful."

Henry Lee's parrot, whose name was Charlie, seemed oblivious to the heated discussion between his new owners, even if the outcome might send him back to the Humane Society. He just continued to sidestep back and forth on Henry Lee's shoulder while randomly repeating "Ahoy, Matey. Ahoy, Matey," and occasionally stopping his pacing to peck at Henry Lee's earlobe, something his new owner thought might pass for bird love.

"OK, I will admit Charlie is not as nasty as outdoor birds," Mary Anne finally conceded, "but I do know for a fact that birds relieve themselves frequently, and they don't really care where it goes." She directed her gaze at Charlie who was staring blankly in her direction. "And if you don't believe me, I'd suggest you double-check that potty-trained claim against the impressive pile of bird doo on your shoulder." She couldn't help but smile when she said it.

"What are you talking about?" Henry Lee said, quickly coaxing the bird onto his right hand so he could pull the shirt fabric away from his shoulder. "Jesus H. Christ, Mary Anne, get me a paper towel," he said, trying to sound amused rather than annoyed. Mary Anne left the room still chuckling and returned with a roll of paper towels. She reeled off a sheet and handed it to Henry Lee.

"And that's another thing," she said while Henry Lee dabbed at his shirt, "I do worry about how parrots repeat everything they hear. Just how long do you think it will be before he starts saying 'Jesus H. Christ' over and over instead of 'Ahoy, Matey'? I'd bet not very long. I can't think of anything more embarrassing than to have your bird go off on a Jesus H. Christ tear with a house full of friends, some certainly more Christian than us."

"Good God, Mary Anne," Henry Lee said in exasperation as he walked out of the kitchen to take Charlie back to his cage, "this bird is not that smart. It takes time to train a parrot. He's not a tape recorder, for God's sake."

"Really," Mary Anne said, "so you know this for a fact, like you knew for a fact he was house-trained?" Henry didn't respond to the sarcasm and just left the kitchen muttering a mild obscenity to himself. The truth was, he didn't know anything about parrot training, but if it somehow turned out that Charlie was some kind of avian savant then Charlie's home visit would be a short one.

Henry Lee's visit to the shelter that day had been a confluence of circumstances, some of which he had control over and others he did not. Certainly, he had no control over the fact that it was a beautiful day, a meteorological happenstance key to his decision to pull the protective cover off his prized 1967 Bonneville convertible and drive it to the mini-mart. And he certainly had no control over the timing of Alfred's death, the family's beloved dog. Alfred had died a year earlier, and the idea of replacing him was one of the key factors that had prompted Henry Lee to visit the Greenwood Humane Society, mainly just to see what it had to offer. However, from then on, the decisions that Henry Lee made were pretty much his own.

On this particular day, he was feeling grateful and free in his classic convertible, a present he had given himself on his fortieth birthday. Based on size alone, he considered the Bonneville something of a private holiday island, an indestructible, chrome-plated, white-walled, lipstick-red monument to the glory days of US manufacturing. The car never failed to draw admiration and perhaps a little envy when he drove it down Green Street.

For the most part, he took out his Bonneville only on warm spring and fall days, although he occasionally drove it to Wrightsville Beach with Mary Anne. He always took less-traveled secondary roads on the trip, winding along byways that cut through tall greening stalks of corn and vast fields of soybeans. The route was more relaxing and intimate than taking the interstate, and the isolation of the drive made them feel like newlyweds, alone and unencumbered and anxious to get to their ocean view hotel room.

Henry Lee's Bonneville also made regular appearances in the annual Greenwood Christmas Parade. The mayor and his wife, Bobby and Belinda Small, preferred waving to the crowds from it, but occasionally some other local celebrity got dibs on the car, perhaps that year's homecoming queen or on a few occasions Hamilton Green and his family. This was likely because Hamilton's great-great-grandfather, Lester Hamilton Green, founded the town more than one hundred and forty years ago, a prideful justification many people thought, unjustly or not was the only reason Hamilton liked to make these public appearances.

One year Santa Claus himself sat on the top of the back seat and threw out handfuls of candy to cheering crowds of children, but Henry Lee vowed not to do that again when he'd found a melted chocolate candy under the driver's seat.

Alfred loved riding in the Bonneville, and over the years the clever dog developed a sixth sense about when his owner was even considering taking out his classic car. He'd start barking and begging whenever Henry Lee reached into the bowl of keys at the front door, hoping to convince his owner to pick out the Bonneville keys. It was never clear how Alfred knew a Bonneville key from a Silverado key, but he did.

When Lester did pick out the Bonneville key, Alfred would run out to the garage to wait patiently for Henry Lee to arrive. Then, once inside, he'd sit by the car's passenger door while Henry Lee removed the protective cloth cover, whimpering with anticipation until his owner could throw a thick blanket over the pristine cream-colored leather passenger seat.

Because Alfred was a mutt, a mix of corgi, dachshund, and beagle, he always needed Henry Lee's help getting onto the seat where he would sit perfectly still as if waiting for a seat belt to be put around him. No wonder Henry Lee's friends and neighbors asked after Alfred with such interest and concern, as if they were checking in on Mary Anne or one of his three children, Henry Lee Jr., Martha Ann, and Travis.

On his way to the store, Henry Lee hadn't seen the handmade signs pointing the way to the annual Greenwood Humane Society Adoption Fair. However, he did notice the signage on his way home, and on a whim, and also full of nostalgic feelings for Alfred, decided to follow a trail of pink and orange poster board signs to the society's new facility a mile or so from downtown.

Usually, pet adoption fairs were chaotic affairs, the air charged with the squeals of excited children and the emotions of anxious parents trying to calm their offspring down. But Henry Lee arrived during a lull in the excitement, so that he ended up with his own personal pet concierge. He warned the volunteer, a pretty high school senior named Tracy, that he was "just looking" and wasn't interested in adopting another dog just yet. Tracy stuck with him anyway and managed to convince him to walk a half-dozen expectant dogs, each one seemingly saying, "Choose me, choose me" with their sad, pleading eyes. It was hard not to adopt them all, but Henry Lee ultimately confessed to Tracy that none of them "felt right," noting that a dog like Alfred was "hard to replace." That's when Tracy used a redirection tactic that old-hand department store salespeople use when they sense a customer's interest is waning after learning their particular size of a pair of pants they came to buy was out of stock, that is, offer them a "perfect shirt" from a nearby rack that goes nicely with the pants they were currently wearing.

"Hey, I know what you need: a talking parrot," Tracy said smiling, "and you're in luck today. We've got a beautiful one that needs a new home. Wanna see him?" Henry Lee still cannot explain his response, even after replaying the conversation over and over in his head dozens of times.

"Sure, why don't you show him to me?" Henry Lee said, so surprised by his response he felt compelled to joke with Tracy that he was considering becoming a pirate and needed a bird to go with his outfit.

"Great, right this way," Tracy chirped, happy with her success "We keep him inside. He's really cute!"

Henry Lee learned at some point in their conversation that Tracy planned to major in marketing in college. "Somehow that doesn't surprise me," Henry Lee told her, although he said it without a hint of irony or sarcasm and more as a statement of fact.

Charlie's cage was nearly the size of a refrigerator box. It was pushed up against the wall across from the reception desk and covered with a brightly colored bedsheet. "All this activity makes him nervous," Tracy told Henry Lee as she walked toward the cage, "but you're welcome to come over and meet him." She yanked at one corner of the sheet with the theatrical flourish of a magician, and the fabric fell away revealing a brilliantly colored parrot perched on a realistic-looking tree limb.

"Charlie, this is Henry Lee," Tracy said.

At first, Charlie simply chirped a few times, perhaps clearing his throat. Then he said, "Ahoy, Matey," followed by a few more short chirps.

Henry Lee laughed out loud. "I'll be," he said, "I was only kidding about becoming a pirate."

"Oh, that's just one of the things he can say," Tracy told Henry Lee. "His former owner was an actual sea captain who took Charlie on his trips around the world. Unfortunately, his owner, Captain Jack, had a stroke so he can't take care of him anymore. His son, who lives here in Greenwood, asked us to find him a new home."

Tracy took Charlie out of his cage and placed him on Henry Lee's shoulder. The bird walked back and forth, unafraid of his potential new owner. "Well, I guess now that I have a parrot on my shoulder, I'll have to follow through on becoming a pirate," Henry Lee said.

Tracy laughed. "I think you'd make a great pirate," she said a bit coquettishly.

Tracy was really good at this, Henry Lee thought.

"Three bells. Three bells," Charlie said, joining in on the conversation, "Full speed ahead. Full speed ahead."

Henry Lee filled out Charlie's pet paperwork that day and met with an adoption coordinator. He arranged for a home visit and set up a trial adoption period of two weeks. After that, if things went well, Charlie would officially become the new Daniel family pet. On his way home, he worked out where he'd keep Charlie. Clearly, the oversize cage would have to stay in the garage. He thought Charlie would be good company when he worked on his car or carried out some other home project. He knew a parrot could not replace Alfred, but he figured a talking bird would still be entertaining to have around.

Inside the house, Henry Lee thought Charlie would be the happiest in the large, vaulted sunroom. He'd have to buy a new cage, but he felt Charlie would like to live among Mary Anne's numerous tropical plants. As for Mary Anne's acceptance of Charlie, he couldn't imagine her not at least finding Charlie endearing (that hadn't exactly gone to plan). Caring for a parrot rather than a dog was also something he thought would argue in Charlie's favor, an important selling point because they had both gotten used to taking longer vacations without worrying about Alfred.

Despite her initial resistance to Charlie's natural habits, Mary Anne eventually was convinced to adopt the homeless parrot, but with a few caveats. Principally, Charlie could fly free only when he was in the garage. And when he was inside the house, he'd have to stay in his new cage or remain perched on Henry Lee's shoulder. She did leave open the possibility of more freedom once she was convinced Charlie would "behave himself."

Apparently, Charlie got the message about behaving himself, and after a month without a single accident on Henry Lee's shoulder or anywhere else, he was allowed to spend hours outside his cage on a new perch nestled among Mary Anne's jungle of potted tropical plants, ferns, palms, bromeliads, philodendrons, schefferas, and even a few bird-of-paradise plants.

Even among all the greenery and slightly hidden behind a large ficus tree, Charlie stood out like a lighthouse, his yellow and red feathers reflecting the sun's afternoon light as he sidestepped back and forth on his perch. When he chirped, as he did constantly, the effect was magical and made Mary Anne imagine she had a bit of the rainforest in the Daniel family's sunroom.

Once he was officially adopted, life with Charlie fell into a comfortable pattern of pet care. In some ways life with Charlie was no different than it had been with Alfred. After making his morning coffee and pulling Charlie's nighttime sheet away from his cage, Henry Lee would say good morning and offer his bare hand to Charlie through the cage door. Charlie always hopped on quickly, anxious to get to his jungle. Most mornings Charlie would respond to his unveiling with "Ahoy, Matey," to which Henry Lee responded with an uncharacteristic lilt of playfulness in his voice, "Ahoy to you too, Matey."

For her part, Mary Anne did come around to thinking Charlie was "cute" and on her best days she would, if asked, concede she enjoyed having Charlie around. "He is a pretty bird for sure," she told her best friend Jolene one day, sitting in her kitchen after one of their weekly power walks through the neighborhood, "and he's been less trouble than I thought, but I don't want to encourage Henry Lee too much. There's no telling what he might drag home next." She grabbed Jolene's arm in the way female friends do when they make jokes about their husbands. They cackled together, both feeling fortunate for having good-hearted, faithful husbands who made life interesting.

Then, about a year after his adoption, Charlie decided he needed a vacation. At least, that is how Henry Lee usually begins the story of Charlie's escape and eventual capture some five miles east of town. "Yep, old Charlie just decided the landlubber's life was not for him," Henry Lee might say. Or he'd say, "So, Charlie just took it on himself to head back to the sea."

Charlie's escape from Henry Lee's garage was a predictable outcome of the trust Henry Lee put in his new pet. At first, Charlie stayed in his oversize cage while Henry Lee worked on projects in his garage. Despite this confinement, he seemed to enjoy the fresh air and change of scenery. After a time, Henry Lee began to completely trust Charlie, and he allowed his pet more time out of his cage to explore the garage. At first, Charlie sat on a perch attached to his cage. Later he perched on a length of half-inch dowel that Henry Lee hung from the garage ceiling rafters by two long strands of heavy copper wire.

From his new vantage point above Henry Lee's workbench, Charlie paid keen attention to whatever Henry Lee was fixing: a ceramic plate, a malfunctioning toaster, his favorite fishing reel. After a time, Henry Lee began training Charlie to offer affirming phrases for his work, mainly because he thought his neighborhood buddies would appreciate the joke of him having a pet parrot encouraging his work.

"What do you think, Charlie?" Henry Lee would ask, holding up a newly repaired clock or blender. "Am I a genius or what?"

"Aye, Matey," Charlie would say, "you fixed it. Aye, you fixed it." Charlie would then chirp and do a victory dance on his perch. Henry Lee's neighborhood friends, whether they were advising him on a repair or more likely just passing the time drinking Henry Lee's beer, chuckled at Charlie's antics, no matter how many times they'd seen him perform.

After a few months of freedom, Charlie took it on himself to expand his territory and flew up to the garage's rafters. The first few times he did this, Henry Lee had to use a ladder to retrieve Charlie. That was a burdensome ritual, so Henry Lee trained Charlie to fly down from his perch and land on his crooked arm when he said, "Let's go, Charlie."

"On the way, Matey," Charlie would reply before swooping down from the rafters like a bird of prey.

Then one day Henry Lee trusted Charlie too much. He left both garage doors open, as he sought relief from the oppressive heat of a summer afternoon and assumed, incorrectly, that Charlie would never even think of escaping. In Henry Lee's defense, nothing about Charlie's behavior that day was unusual, despite the gaping path to freedom not twenty yards from his perch. Charlie even offered Henry Lee encouragement several times that day from his rafter perch as he worked on a pump from Mary Anne's garden fountain. "Aye, you fixed it, Matey," he called down from above.

9 – Henry Lee's Bird

Truthfully, the pump's tiny magnet had been reduced to a solid ball of copper because that's what happens when a water pump tries to pump air. Henry Lee had thanked Charlie anyway.

In retrospect, Henry Lee should have closed the garage doors before calling Charlie to come down from the rafters. He could have simply closed the garage doors and let Charlie fly free while he went downtown to the Greenwood Hardware and Supply Company to buy a new pump from his friend Stewart Peabody. Unfortunately, Henry Lee didn't follow through on these prudent safety measures and instead crooked his right arm and called up to Charlie, "Let's go, Matey," expecting Charlie to fly right down.

He should have known something was not right. Charlie didn't acknowledge his call, something that rarely happened. Instead, Charlie sidestepped nervously on his perch twelve feet above the garage floor. Henry Lee called nearly a half-dozen times before Charlie fluttered his wings and dove like a kamikaze pilot toward Henry Lee's outstretched arm. Then, right in the middle of this familiar trajectory, Charlie veered left and flew straight out the garage door and was gone.

"Jesus H. Christ," Henry Lee swore as he watched Charlie fly toward the blue, cloudless sky. "Let's go. Let's go. Let's go," he called.

Nothing.

"Charlie, let's go. Let's go, goddammit!" Henry Lee called repeatedly as he ran down his driveway and out into the street, "Charlie, let's go."

Standing still in the middle of his street, Henry Lee heard no chirps at all. Nothing but the sound of a summer breeze rustling through the tall oak, maple, and walnut trees that surrounded Henry Lee's backyard. In the distance, he heard the muted sound of a running lawn mower mingled with the annoying whine of an electric leaf blower two streets over. And although he can't swear to it, Henry Lee could have sworn he heard someone, perhaps Charlie, mock his strident signature profanity: "Je-SUS H. Christ! Je-SUS H. Christ!"

Henry Lee first tried putting up missing pet posters on every telephone pole within a reasonable radius of his home. Just like every other escaped or lost pet poster, whether dog, cat, snake, guinea pig, or pet iguana, the poster featured a picture of the missing pet, in this case a photo of Charlie with a caption underneath that read as follows.

> MISSING PARROT
> If Seen
> Please Call Number Below
> Goes by the Name Charlie
> Friendly and Talkative
> 555-389-9943
> Henry Lee Daniel
> 108 Taylor Farm Road

He knew this method was a long shot based on his own experience of never personally spotting any of the missing animals featured in any of these ubiquitous posters. He knew he had to recruit a larger contingent of searchers because Charlie had a big advantage over other escapees: He could fly.

Fortunately, Henry Lee had his own advantage over ordinary citizens who had lost their pet cat or dog. He had a good friend who worked at the local newspaper, the *Greenwood Clarion*, as the advertising manager. It was a connection that put him in a position to meet with the paper's feature editor, Max Perkins, who knew a good human interest story when he saw one. It also helped that Max owned a couple of parakeets himself.

The story, published a few days after Max's interview with Henry Lee, was accompanied by a three-column, tightly framed photo of Charlie perched on Henry Lee's shoulder pecking at his ear. The forty-eight-point headline read, "Ahoy, Matey: Reward Offered for This Seafaring Parrot." The idea of offering a reward was the feature editor's idea because he thought it would bring more attention to the article.

It took a few days for the story to percolate through the community, but when it did, the calls came in a torrent. It seemed like everyone in town had seen Charlie whether they lived north, south, east, or west of town. It was a diversity of directions that made Henry Lee think there had been a sudden parrot invasion in Greenwood, or perhaps the reward money was not such a good idea after all.

Still, the story got the community talking about Charlie's fate so that friends and sometimes strangers asked Henry Lee how the search for Charlie was going. Eventually, about four days after the article was published, he got a call from Sy Blanding who said he'd noticed a colorful bird perched on the wind pennant of a sailboat he was restoring in his backyard.

"Yeah," Sy told Henry Lee, "he's a pretty bird. Not like any bird I've seen before. And he won't leave my boat even though I've tried to shoo him away. He is making a mess of my deck. I read the article in the paper, and then I heard him say, 'Ahoy Matey' this morning, and that's when I knew he must be your pet parrot."

Henry Lee, for reasons he cannot explain, ran to his garage, pulled the protective cover off his Bonneville, and backed it out into the street. Then he went inside to retrieve Charlie's cage from the sunroom jungle and secured it in the front seat of his car with a bungee cord. Typically, Henry Lee never exceeded the speed limit in his Bonneville, but this was an emergency. He gunned his precious classic car and nearly scraped its pristine underside as he bumped over his driveway's apron. It was a sound he'd never have ignored under normal circumstances, but on this day he felt nothing but his worry about Charlie.

It took less than fifteen minutes to drive to Sy Blanding's house just south of downtown. Sy's house, a typical 1970s split-level, was situated on a two-acre plot with plenty of room for a backyard sailboat restoration project. Sy came out within a few minutes of Henry Lee's arrival and predictably began asking about his car before realizing why the shiny classic car was in his driveway in the first place.

"I guess you want to see if I have your pet bird in my backyard," Sy said. "Sorry, I got sidetracked."

"That's OK," Henry Lee said, unconcerned, "I'm used to it. She is a beauty for sure."

Sy told Henry Lee he should drive around to his backyard to get closer to his sailboat, a twenty-five-foot craft that had seen better days. Henry Lee parked his Bonneville next to the boat, turned off the engine, and then looked up apprehensively, fearing Charlie might fly away. He nearly cried when he saw his pet sidestepping and chirping on the wind pennant. It was a hopeful feeling soon supplanted by fear, a feeling not unlike the terror he felt when one of his own children got too close to the edge of any abyss. *Good God*, he thought, *how is it that some hawk has not had you for lunch already?* He started calling for Charlie even before he got out of his car.

"Let's go, Charlie. Let's go. Let's go," Henry repeated, as loudly as he could manage.

At first, Charlie didn't seem to hear Henry Lee. Then, suddenly, he flew off his perch straight for his owner's arm, landing with a force that broke the skin. Henry Lee hadn't really thought about what to do once Charlie flew back to him. He could have asked Sy to throw a sheet over Charlie to make sure he didn't fly away again. Or he might have considered gently clapping his left hand over Charlie while he wrapped his right hand around him in some firm but harmless way.

He did none of that. Instead, he coaxed Charlie onto his left index finger, walked him straight back to the Bonneville, and opened the cage he'd brought from the sunroom. Charlie waited patiently while Henry Lee slid open the cage door and happily returned to his perch inside as if today was no different than any other. Henry Lee nearly cried again as he locked the cage door, but somehow managed to avoid that embarrassment.

Henry Lee and Sy engaged in a short conversation about the search for Charlie and how happy Henry Lee was to have Charlie back. They also had another conversation about the challenges of boat and car restoration projects. Eventually, Henry Lee pulled two, one-hundred-dollar bills from his shirt pocket and extended his hand toward Sy, the two bills wedged between his middle and index fingers.

"Here ya go, I really appreciate you helping me find Charlie," Henry Lee said.

"Oh, that's OK, I'm just happy to help. Don't need a reward."

"No, you should take it," Henry Lee said. "I mean, if not for Charlie finding your sailboat, I don't think we'd ever have seen him again."

"Well, if you insist," Sy said. "I'll add it to the restoration fund. It's a work in progress."

"Looks like it," Henry Lee said, trying not to sound judgmental.

Henry Lee thanked Sy again, then secured the seat belt around Charlie's cage. He started the Bonneville and crept back toward Sy's paved driveway through a patch of tall grass, worried that there might be hidden rocks. Once back on the driveway, he raised a hand above his head to say goodbye to Charlie's rescuer as he drove down the long strip of black asphalt driveway toward the main road.

"Well, Charlie," Henry Lee said as he turned homeward, "did you have a nice adventure?"

"Aye, Matey," Charlie answered. "You fixed it, Matey. You fixed it."

"I did fix it, Charlie," Henry Lee said, delighted by Charlie's insight. "You're right about that."

Mary Anne was waiting in their driveway when he returned. She cheered and cried when she saw that Charlie was safe. "Ahoy, Matey," she said, "glad to have you home."

"Aye, Matey," Charlie chirped. She held the front door open and walked beside Charlie's cage all the way to her sunroom where she helped Henry Lee get Charlie situated on his perch behind her ficus tree.

"You know, we were lucky to get Charlie back," Mary Anne confessed that night over dinner. "But we should take him to the vet just to make sure he's OK."

"I can do that," Henry Lee said.

"And while you're there, have him checked to see if he's picked up any mites and such," she added. It was a theme, Henry Lee thought, so he just said "surely" and left it at that.

After dinner they both visited Charlie's cage to officially welcome him home. Mary Anne pushed a piece of apple through the cage bars. Charlie took the gift and chirped with delight.

"So, Charlie," Henry Lee said, "you and I are going to see the vet tomorrow. Is that OK with you?"

Charlie dropped the piece of apple and began nervously side-stepping on his perch.

"What's wrong, Charlie?" Henry Lee asked. "Don't you want to go to the vet?"

Charlie chirped two or three times, then replied, "Je-SUS H. Christ, Matey! Je-SUS H. Christ!"

"Well, I'll be, Charlie must have been practicing while he was on his vacation," Henry Lee quipped, looking directly at Mary Anne. "I guess you want to send him back to the Humane Society now?"

"Of course not," Mary Anne replied, "but he'll have to stay in the garage the next time we have a party."

"That will be fine with Charlie," Henry Lee said. He looked directly at his profanity-prone pet. "Is that all right, Charlie, you won't mind it, will you?"

Charlie chirped something he took for agreement.

Henry Lee shook out an old bedsheet, covered Charlie's cage, and turned off the lights as he left the room.

"Good night, Charlie," he said.

His pet didn't respond, but then Charlie had been on quite an adventure, even for a well-traveled, seafaring parrot, and he needed his rest.

10

Milton Gets His Freedom

AS THE REGIONAL SALES MANAGER FOR THE Reynolds Tobacco Company, Bentley Thomas traveled to Raleigh every other week, so planning a road trip with his grandson was just a matter of scheduling his time and convincing his grandson's mother, Martha Ann McCarthy, that her son would return home unharmed and uncorrupted.

Martha Ann's irrational fear that something unforeseen and tragic might happen to her son, Milton, was something Bentley had discussed with his daughter on several occasions. At best, his council elicited nothing more than tepid promises that she would "begin letting go" when some maturity milestone—age or grade level—was crossed. These waypoints were, of course, a moving target, and he often worried that his grandson was well on his way to becoming a momma's boy, something he wouldn't stand for, even if the well-intentioned momma was his own daughter.

Bentley normally scheduled his regional office meetings with his boss, the regional sales director, as early as possible to avoid late afternoon traffic when he drove back to Greenwood. However, for this trip with his grandson, he scheduled only a late-morning meeting, which would give him time to show Milton a few downtown landmarks and the neighborhood where Bentley grew up. He told Milton that having these places in his head would "help him get his bearings should he get lost."

"It's always important to know where you are in order to get where you're going," he told Milton as they discussed plans for the day. Milton's lack of orienteering skills was chiefly due to his mother's refusal to let him join the Scouts or even go camping with his grandfather for fear her only son might be attacked by a black bear, bitten by a rattlesnake, or get a deadly parasite from drinking spring water. Still, Milton acknowledged his grandfather's advice as if he understood, moving his head up and down, and mumbling something that sounded like acquiescence.

Bentley knew just about every street in the city, having grown up just a few blocks east of the capitol in a neighborhood called Oakwood. His ancestral home, a large Victorian built by his grandfather, is listed on the National Register of Historic Places and is known widely in the area as the Thomas House. Tourists and even locals sometimes slow down to take pictures from their car windows of the pristinely restored home. Some even take time to pull off the wide, tree-lined boulevard to read a placard describing the house's history that is attached to a surrounding wrought iron fence.

This extra scrutiny of Bentley's childhood home happened mostly these days when his mother's hydrangea bushes—or descendants of them —were in bloom, each bush a bursting riot of pink, purple, and white blossoms the size of a wedding bouquet. The band of flower bushes around the house sometimes made Bentley think of the flower crowns that had encircled his sister's head when she left the house to attend the annual May Day celebrations in the neighborhood.

When Bentley was Milton's age, his mother shooed him and his two brothers out the front door in the morning with mock irritation, telling them she didn't want to see them again until suppertime. Despite such neglect, they all survived the worst of adolescent stupidity, including tempting tragic consequences by riding their bikes in and out of downtown traffic as if playing car dodgeball.

After surviving that test of immortality, they would race one another to the capitol grounds, drop their bikes on the cool grass, and sprawl their sweaty bodies under the same ancient oak tree where he now intended to leave his grandson on his own to explore the grounds. Bentley's hope, as fanciful as it seemed, was that some residual of his own spirit of fearlessness, and perhaps stupidity at times, might have seeped into the surrounding soil and would, like an ancient warrior's ghost, rise up to inhabit Milton's sheltered heart.

On their drive from Greenwood, Bentley asked questions as if Milton were applying for the job of grandson, asking how he liked school, who his friends were, what he did in his free time, what books he read, and what he wanted to do when he grew up. He didn't bother to ask if Milton had a girlfriend because he felt he already knew the answer. His grandson's answers confirmed that Milton had indeed led a fearful and sheltered life thus far, a fact that further convinced him he needed to set his grandson free.

As it turned out, less than a year after their road trip, Martha Ann announced she was pregnant with a "surprise" child—a blessed event even though she was nearly forty. The arrival of a new brother did eventually turn his mother's attention elsewhere, but Milton

10 – Milton Gets His Freedom

didn't have time to wait for such an excruciatingly slow process of maturation to get him out from under his mother's thumb.

At the time of Milton's visit, his grandfather's childhood neighborhood was still "undiscovered," the homes having mostly gone to seed after residents abandoned the neighborhood for newer, more convenient homes in the suburbs with sparkling modern shopping centers, better schools (code at the time for no people of color), and reliable, upgraded infrastructure. Still, he drove respectfully down Oakwood's wide streets beneath a canopy of century-old oaks that so darkened the brilliant blue sky above them that Bentley was forced to remove his sunglasses.

As he approached the home he had grown up in, Bentley slowed and depressed the clutch while at the same time slipping the steering column shifter into neutral. He allowed the car to roll silently to a stop directly in front of 304 Magnolia Boulevard. At the time of Milton's first visit, the building was more impressive for its size than its state of repair. Although seeing the home in such a condition was painful, Bentley did his best to create a mental picture for Milton of the home he had known more than forty years ago.

Bentley described how his mother and two helpers worked constantly to maintain the nearly one acre of gardens, noting that the grounds had always been the envy of the neighborhood. He described the home's grand staircase and his grandfather's mahogany-paneled library with its rows of leather-bound books, each with a gold-embossed title on the spine. He told Milton how it felt to sit on a cushioned porch swing waiting for a cool breeze to chase away the oppressive summer heat.

These historical abstractions didn't initially hold the attention of a fourteen-year-old boy given the irresistible draw of his grandfather's generous backseat littered with sample cigarette packages, customer order books, and affinity tchotchkes, such as key chains, pens, and logoed baseball caps. To this day, Milton still has stored somewhere in his garage a key chain and a faded, sweat-stained hat with the letters RJR embossed on the bill.

Fortunately, Bentley was a natural-born, infectious storyteller. He had a rare ability to marshal an impressive array of salient facts in his head, paste them onto a mental wallboard, and flawlessly assemble them on the fly into well-constructed, cogent sentences that he presented seamlessly and with all due dramatic affectation as if he were reading from a teleprompter. Milton was soon enthralled by his grandfather's eloquence, and he had questions about every house they passed, often begging for more details than Bentley had at hand.

"Who lived in that one?" Milton asked when they passed a particularly large, dilapidated Victorian with four turrets and a widow's walk in the center of the towering roof.

"Oh, that's an interesting one," his grandfather told him. "That one belonged to the Messner family. Granby Messner, the father, was president of the largest bank in town. We were not related to them, but I once attended a party there for his daughter Jasmine when I was about your age. I remember we were served red velvet cake on fine bone china plates with gold inlay around the edges. The family crest, as I remember, was a golden-horned Scottish stag embossed in the center of each plate, saucer, and bowl."

"The lemonade was made right in front of us on an elegant mahogany sideboard and served in crystal goblets that one of the family's helpers, all of whom wore white gloves, placed on the table in front of us just so. The goblet was so heavy, I had to use two hands to pick it up.

"It was my first formal dinner," he continued, adding an extra measure of Southern drawl, "and all the pomp and circumstance of it made me nervous, so much so that when I reached across the table for a biscuit, which was served in a polished silver breadbasket and covered by a stiff, white linen napkin, I knocked over my crystal glass and broke it—two things you weren't supposed to do at a formal dinner: reach across the table or break expensive glassware. The uniformed help cleaned it all up and told me not to worry about it, but I was never asked back to their house again, although I'm sure my father insisted on replacing the goblet after I told him about my social faux pas. In any case, I can assure you I have never made those two mistakes of etiquette again."

Looking back on his grandfather's neighborhood tour, it seemed to Milton that just about every house they passed had a story, some tragic and some humorous enough to make him laugh out loud. He especially liked stories about his relatives, many "gone to their reward" as Bentley characterized their passing in a tone that belied a subtlety of meaning, somewhere between ridicule and longing for it to be true.

"That house," Bentley said, pointing to a smaller, slightly rundown bungalow with a generous front porch and an ugly wheelchair ramp defacing the yard, "now that house was where my Aunt Lizzy lived. She was quite a character and a good soul, really. She claimed she had a gift for helping people understand their dreams like a fortune teller."

"Really?" Melvin said.

"Well, I don't know if it was true or not, but a lot of folks back then thought so," Bentley said.

"She kept what she called her books of dreams where all the dreams she'd ever had were recorded and organized by year. These were mostly written in spiral-bound notebooks like the ones you use in school, although in her later years she recorded her dreams in nicely bound leather ones as well. Unfortunately, I suspect all her books were just thrown away when she died, which is a shame.

"In any case, sometimes I would ride my bike over to visit," Bentley said, pointing at the ruined house. "And occasionally I'd ask Aunt Lizzy to get one of her notebooks and read her dreams to me while we sat in the big, white, rocking chairs she said had once belonged to her grandfather. I have forgotten the details of what she read to me, but I do remember one dream she had about a young man who went off to war and returned to marry a golden-haired beauty, despite nearly all of his friends dying in battle. And guess what? That really came true. I did join the Army during World War Two, some of my best friends did die in battle, and I did come back to marry your grandmother, and she was indeed a golden-haired beauty."

"Is that really true?" Melvin asked.

"Sure," his grandfather answered, "and even if it's just mostly true, what's important, at least in storytelling, is that you never let the truth get in the way of a good story, as someone once said."

After leaving Oakwood, Bentley drove the few blocks to downtown where he showed Melvin new and old landmark buildings as if he were the mayor giving dignitaries a tour. He pointed out a recently built bank building, famous or formally famous hotels, restaurants, and movie theaters, sites of long-disappeared nightclubs, and occasionally an empty parking lot where an iconic Beaux-Arts or Art Deco style building had once stood. Milton noticed that much of his grandfather's commentary about the places, people, and incidents he described began or ended with a variation of the qualifier, "when I was your age," something his grandfather said created verisimilitude for the listener.

"It's a literary expression that I suspect you'll learn in school someday," his grandfather told him when asked about its meaning, "but for now let's just say verisimilitude is the details you put in a story to make your audience care about listening to it."

After the city tour, Bentley parked his car in a nearby garage, and he and Milton walked the few blocks to the capitol grounds. The two took their time, walking so slowly in fact that other well-dressed adults who seemed to be in a hurry to be somewhere important were forced to swerve around them.

Such city buzz and frenetic activity was a world away from Greenwood, where the tallest structure was the old Harrison Price Hotel on Main Street. Generations of Greenwood High School students walked through that building's front doors and marveled at its formally elegant grand entrance hall on their way to a prom or cotillion where they danced and sweated the night away on the formally elegant, scuffed, and faded parquet ballroom floor.

"So, buddy," Bentley asked his grandson as they threaded their way through the pedestrians, "you think you can manage on your own while I go to my meeting?"

"Yes, sir," Milton said with more confidence than he actually felt.

"That's it," his grandfather said, firmly gripping Milton's shoulder with a strong, confident hand. "I am not worried about you one little bit." A mostly true statement, Bentley thought.

Bentley got so hot on his walk to the capitol building that he removed his well-pressed jacket (something he hardly ever did, no matter how hot he got) and flung it over his shoulder nonchalantly. Once on the capitol grounds, Bentley and Milton found a granite bench positioned under a massive live oak branch and sat down. Bentley draped his jacket over his lap, a white linen seersucker that was now beginning to wrinkle, and placed his hat, a white Panama with a red hatband, next to him. Then he rested a reassuring hand on Milton's bare knee and gave him a final dose of encouragement before leaving him alone for the next few hours to explore the grounds.

"There's plenty to do around here," Bentley said, gesturing expansively with his hand. "The capitol itself is more than a hundred years old. You can take a tour of it if you'd like. Then there's the North Carolina Museum of History over in that direction." He pointed directly behind Milton and waited for him to turn around and follow his finger's line of sight. "You can't see it from here, but it's a big building like the capitol. It's hard to miss. You'll find lots of interesting exhibits there. In fact, I think the museum could easily keep you occupied all morning."

Bentley pulled out a palm full of dimes, nickels, and quarters from his still perfectly pressed pants pocket and offered them to his grandson. "Here, take these," he said. "You can buy yourself a snack if you want, and remember, if you run into any trouble, you can't solve yourself, call me at this number." He gave Milton a business card with a phone number written on the back in neat block script. "That's where I'll be, but I don't suspect you'll need me. You'll be fine."

Bentley stood up, straightened his red bowtie, slipped on his jacket, and put on his hat. He turned to walk away but then hesitated to dramatically twist his body to face Melvin again. "Oh, and here's one last thing," he said. "I want you to meet me at this exact spot precisely at noon. Not a minute later. Can you do that?"

"I can," Milton said confidently, holding out his arm and tapping his new watch with his right-hand index finger. "You can count on me."

"I'm sure of it," said his grandfather. Bentley then walked away without a single backward glance.

10 – Milton Gets His Freedom

At first Milton wandered aimlessly, even nervously, around the grounds, looking up at the statues and reading commemorative plaques. None of the names, events, or commemorations were familiar to him except of course the towering monument to the Civil War dead. That was a historical event he definitely knew about. Years later Milton would develop a near obsession with reading historical placards, something that compelled him to pull off the road to read them, an activity that drew him into imagining what had happened there, and if something did, whether it might be a good story to tell. Had he not gone to his own reward, Bentley surely would have been pleased with how Milton turned out, especially for the way he now fearlessly explored the world.

Milton considered following his grandfather's sightseeing advice but changed his mind when he learned that the state's legislative branch had moved to a new building some distance away in 1963. Just the idea of looking at empty chairs where politicians once sat sounded as boring as listening in on the dinner conversations of his parents and their friends. Instead, he set out across the grounds to find the museum his grandfather had pointed out. He was pleased when he found it easily, an early success on his journey to becoming a lifelong curious traveler.

In the museum's lobby, a docent wearing a bright red vest noticed Milton as he stood slack-jawed looking up in wonder at the vaulted lobby ceiling. The docent, a white-haired, cheery retiree with a museum badge resting nonchalantly on the ledge of his endearing paunch, walked over and introduced himself as Mr. Hanson. He said he was there to help, and after finding out where Milton was from and how old he was, the docent launched into a detailed description of the museum's current exhibitions. To the ears of an adolescent boy, with a buzz cut and the beginnings of teenage acne, each exhibit sounded more boring than the next. Then Mr. Hanson began describing a new exhibit about the life and times of North Carolina's most famous pirate resident, Blackbeard.

"Really?" Milton said, "Blackbeard the pirate?"

"Yes, really," said the docent. "There's even some gold coins that might have belonged to the pirate himself."

"Really?" he said again.

"Yes, really," the docent repeated. "Sounds to me that's something you'd be interested in seeing."

Mr. Hanson was right, the gold coins did capture Melvin's interest for a time, but ultimately, he judged the Blackbeard exhibit extremely short on *things to see* and way too long on *things to read*, which were mainly faded journals, letters, and other historical documents protected by a thick sheet of clear plexiglass.

Still, the museum did have many other things to hold the interest of any lanky, awkward boy: antique guns, one called a blunderbuss, which resembled a weapon he'd seen Wile E. Coyote use against the Road Runner on Saturday morning cartoons; old cannonballs and spent Civil War bullets; and industrial machinery with dangerous-looking gears whose purpose he could only guess. He wondered what would happen if someone's fingers got caught in the device, proof once again he was too anxious for his own good.

The exhibit that impressed him the most that day was a replica of the 1903 Wright Flyer that the Wright Brothers flew at Kitty Hawk, a history-changing event that proved humans could indeed follow the birds into the sky. He read every placard and studied each aviation relic like a monk viewing a piece of the Holy Cross. Two

10 – Milton Gets His Freedom

hours sped by so quickly that he was nearly ten minutes late meeting his grandfather, even after covering the distance from the museum to their oak tree in a full run.

"What's wrong, somebody chasing you?" his grandfather asked with a chuckle, when Milton arrived, frantic and out of breath.

"No, sir," Milton explained. "I just lost track of time in the museum."

"That's OK, I wasn't too worried about you," his grandfather said, calmly halving, then quartering that day's edition of the *News & Observer*. "After all, you can take care of yourself, can't you?" Milton nodded his head up and down, then relaxed, thankful he hadn't ruined his chances for future adventures with his grandfather.

"I really did like the museum," Milton said enthusiastically, once he had his breath back. "Especially the Wright Brothers airplane, although I'm not sure I'd want to fly in it."

"I've seen it," his grandfather said with a slight chuckle. "If you like that airplane, maybe I'll take you to Washington, DC, sometime to visit the National Air and Space Museum. They have the real Wright Flyer in that museum, along with other airplanes I think you'll like."

"Are you kidding?" Milton said with more excitement than Bentley expected his grandson could muster.

"No, I'm not kidding," Bentley said, "We'll ask your mom when we get home."

Bentley and his grandson went to Washington a few years later after his brother was born. Bentley's daughter didn't object because she was glad to have her slightly surly teenager out of her house for a while. Bentley took a picture of his grandson pointing up to the Wright Flyer hanging from the Air and Space Museum's ceiling, a picture he framed and took with him to college.

"I'm glad you enjoyed yourself," Bentley told Milton as they began walking back to the parking garage.

"I did," Milton said, "although some of it was boring. There was nothing to see in the Blackbeard exhibit except a bunch of old letters and journals under glass."

"That's true," Bentley told his grandson, pausing for a moment while he assembled his next thoughts. "Blackbeard lived a long time ago, and there's not much left of him or the things he owned. After all, he was a criminal who eventually lost his head. But here's the truth about history. It's just another form of storytelling. Most, or at least a significant part of it, is true but it's the skill of those who weave those dry facts together that makes it interesting. Just remember, as with any entertaining story, even the ones I tell, you have to consume them all with a healthy bit of skepticism."

Bentley paused, realizing he had waxed too philosophic for an adolescent boy, so he added, "But I suspect that's something you'll understand when you get older. For now, I'm just glad you enjoyed yourself.

"And by the way," Bentley said to Milton conspiratorially as they made their way around the lunchtime crowds on the sidewalk, "let's not mention your free time today to your mother. It's our secret for now, OK?"

"Sure, Pop," Milton said, feeling strangely grown-up and unencumbered for the first time in his life. "Mum's the word," he said, using an odd-sounding phrase he'd heard his grandfather say on a few occasions.

"Exactly," Bentley said, "mum's the word, at least for now. Besides," he continued, "your adventure today will likely make a good story for your own grandchildren someday. Just remember, they weren't here, so you're allowed to make it interesting. Understand?"

Milton nodded his head in agreement, although he would not completely understand his grandfather's advice until he became a fiction writer known for his always vivid imagination and creative use of facts.

Photo by Bob Carragher

About the Author

MARK MORROW HAS ENJOYED A CAREER AS A journalist, photographer, editor, and author.

His first book, *Images of the Southern Writer* (University of Georgia Press, 1985) was a collection of his Southern writer portraits along with accompanying essays about photographing, and befriending, some of America's most iconic writers.

These writers included Tennessee Williams, Eudora Welty, Walker Percy, Cormac McCarthy, James Dickey, William Styron, Erskine Caldwell, Anne Tyler, and dozens of others. He has also photographed and corresponded with many other writers in his career, including Joseph Heller, Tom Wolfe, Tom Stoppard, Donald Hall, Czesław Miłosz, Roy Blount Jr., Garrison Keillor, Stephen Spender, Isaac Bashevis Singer, Tom T. Hall, Toni Morrison, Tim O'Brien, and Willie Morris.

As a photographer, journalist, and book editor, he has worked for a wide range of publications, including newspapers and magazines and has had assignments for *Esquire, People, Fortune*, the *Los Angeles Times*, and others. He is a former executive editor at McGraw-Hill Professional Publishing.

About the Author

In 2023, the University of South Carolina's Irvin Department of Rare Books and Special Collections in Columbia, South Carolina, accepted Mark's entire collection of photographs, letters, and all associated material related to his career as a photographer and writer into its permanent collection. The collection will be archived, catalogued, and eventually made available to the public. The Irvin Collections is planning a late 2024 exhibition of his work. Another major exhibition is planned for the fall of 2025 at Koger Center for the Arts in Columbia, South Carolina.

Mark lives in Alexandria, Virginia, with his wife Tally Tripp.

Printed in the USA
CPSIA information can be obtained
at www.ICGtesting.com
LVHW051441130324
774328LV00007B/782